FLASH GARDENS, AND OTHER SHORT FICTION

(VOLUME ONE)

LOUIS GALLO

ANAPHORA LITERARY PRESS

QUANAH, TEXAS

ANAPHORA LITERARY PRESS
1108 W 3rd Street
Quanah, TX 79252
https://anaphoraliterary.com

Book design by Anna Faktorovich, Ph.D.

Printed in the United States of America, United Kingdom and in Australia on acid-free paper.

Cover Image: Vincent van Gogh's "The Poet's Garden" (1888; Mr. and Mrs. Lewis Larned Coburn Memorial Collection: Art Institute Chicago).

Published in 2023 by Anaphora Literary Press

Flash Gardens, and Other Short Fiction (Volume One)
Louis Gallo—1st edition.

Library of Congress Control Number: 2023912938

Library Cataloging Information
Gallo, Louis, 1945-, author.
    Flash gardens, and other short fiction : Volume one / Louis Gallo
    176 p. ; 9 in.
    ISBN 978-1-68114-599-0 (softcover : alk. paper)
    ISBN 978-1-68114-600-3 (hardcover : alk. paper)
    Kindle (e-book)
1. Literature & Fiction—Short Stories—Single Authors.
2. Literature & Fiction—United States—Short Stories.
3. Literature & Fiction—Literary Fiction—Short Stories.
PN3311-3503: Literature: Prose fiction
813: American fiction in English

CONTENTS

for the usual suspects—Cat, Claire and Maddie

Acknowledgements

Xavier Review: "Degas and the Turkey Buzzard"; StorySouth: "Hector Coquille," "Watermelon Spit": *Flash Fiction*: "Beast in the Jungle"; *Mash Stories*: "Thieves," "Never Start or End a Story with a Dream"; *Fictive Dream*: "Maryjane," "Hunger," "Crème de Menth," "The Arcs of the Covenant," "Pennies and Dandelions," "Honeysuckle and Sweet Olive," "Recruitment, with Bosco," "Bricks," "La Petite Mort," "First Love," "La Belle Dame Sans Merci," "Poetry Reading," "Seduction," "Tyler Avenue," "Off the Road," "Bayou Road," "New Shirt [reprinted in *Best Small Fictions 2020*]"; *Litro*: "Syrbeck"; *Raleigh/ Durham News & Observer*: "The Last Mosquito"; *Thema*: "Dog Day"; *Rosebud*: "General Beauregard," "Bedtime Story"; *Skyline Review*: "Columbus Street"; *Short Story* "Shrine"; *Flash, an International Journal of Flash Fiction*: "Italian"; *Utopia Science Fiction Magazine* "The Theory of Specific Relativity"; *The Fiction Pool*: "This Little Piggie"; *Vocabulary Review*: "Ablative Absolute"; *Rkvry Literary Journal*: "Whitney"; *The Fiction Pool*: "Piano Lesson"; *BioStories*, "Legs"; *Eclectic Flash*: "Spoon?": *Pennsylvania Literary Journal*, "Jonathan Edwards," "Wittgenstein: a Micro-Biography": *Litro*: "Monstrosity," "The Player"; *Floyd County Moonshine*: "Chamber Music" (published as "Vadish"); *Silver Birch Press*: "A Special Case"; *Rockford Review*: "Religious Experience"; *SaLit Magazine*: "Mary"; *Bartleby-Snopes*, "Plutonium"; *The Forge*: "Mama's Boy"; *Pretty Owl Press*: "You're Beautiful."

You're Beautiful

Mars and Venus on a blind date in the Vieux Carré

We're in Galatoire's and I watch you nibble the shrimp remoulade with some regret and not a little nausea. I don't like you. The feeling is mutual but here we are. I invited you because you're beautiful and everyone needs a dose of beauty in the otherwise miasmal cumulus of passing time. What does that say about me? I presume the worst. And though it's my stupid peccadillo, I can't stand to watch girls eat meat of any kind. They should eat flowers that smell heavenly. Hitler said eating meat is eating a corpse. Not that I admire Hitler. They say he loved children and always smelled like soap to disguise his constant gaseous effusions. From here we'll stroll down Bourbon and cut across to the Napoleon House for Ramos Gin Fizzes—or maybe a few shots of yellow chartreuse. Someone will have slid Ravel's Pavane for a Dead Princess onto the ancient turntable, and you will stare at the ceiling. I still don't like you. This is where they sought to sequester Napoleon after his planned rescue from St. Helena's—which didn't work out. And who can decide what's true or false anymore? Maybe I love you, I don't know, but it's pretty feeble to desire someone because they're beautiful. I've met some pretty evil beautiful people. And you just sit there at the table sipping a strawberry daiquiri, that blank look on your face. You hate me. Why are we here together? Napoleon lost Waterloo because his hemorrhoids were flaring, not because Wellington was a better tactician. I don't tell you any of this because you would sigh, smile wanly and blink your eyes. I don't tell you anything. You don't tell me anything. We're miserable. Monet's blue lilies, Van Gogh's Wheat Field with Crows, Goya's Los Desastres de la Guerra… God, you're beautiful.

Tarot: The Fool

We dined on neon wishbones, the soup a flamboyant broth with sugared cucumbers on the side of that stately terrazzo in Paraguay or maybe that time in ancient Cathay when the peasants danced in the street proclaiming a joyous revolution as mandarins clattered their teeth in displeasure. You smiled at me with rococo eyes as we sipped aperitifs in hammocks stretched between eucalyptus trees in Sao Tome—the ham operator tapping SOS on his brass mechanical key. Oh, the island birds clamored in frenzy. We bathed and romped naked in the sulfurous healing springs of West Virginia where Jefferson once sought cure. The allure of blue mountains charmed us into languid serenity, and we bathed too in each other's bodies, liquid in our passion.

Ah, the good life is everywhere, and you are everywhere with me and life is dolce, dolce, a mist of confectioner's sugar. We dreamed our way into the Major Arcana and they still dub us Zero.

General Beauregard

Love had bestirred Miss Yunt's heart with turbulence and uproar back in her late teens, and she never recovered. She had spotted the former Confederate general Pierre Gustave Toutant Beauregard at a Mardi Gras ball sponsored by the Mystick Krewe of Comus and succumbed hopelessly to his magnetism. At this point in his career, having refused lucrative and high ranking offers from the Egyptian and Rumanian armies, Beauregard nestled avidly into his shady position as manager of the Louisiana State Lottery, though legends of his invincibility at Ft. Sumter and Bull Run lived on. No one talked about the fiasco at Shiloh, which Beauregard helped lose by failing to take action. Locals blamed Jefferson Davis whose ill will toward the general was keen and well known. Alas for Miss Yunt, the general was fifty-six years old and she only nineteen, and her father, who noticed fireworks in her eyes, sternly forbade any dalliance with an old fart who ran the lottery. "We are Yunts," he reminded her, "we go back, how far no one cares, but far. We once owned everything, or a lot at any rate. We lost it all, true, but we prosper in memory. Besides, the man has frog blood. No daughter of mine—"

Beauregard too had noticed havoc in the young woman's countenance and might have saved both father and daughter much grief had she only approached him directly rather than mooned from a distance. He had prepared what he imagined a cursory speech to her or anyone else her age who might approach him with affairs of the heart. "Young woman," he would begin, "while your charms are considerable, while your ardor flatters me no end, I must peremptorily decline your entreaties, given my age and propriety. I could be your grandfather, my dear, and something about that most dolorous fact dissuades me from pursuit. I cannot, to be blunt, begin anew at my age. A few years ago perhaps I could have risen to the occasion, loaded it with my best ammunition so to speak, but, alas, time has no mercy. You see me through heroic lenses, the savior of Ft. Sumter—an almost bloodless battle, by the way—a warrior, a dashing general of the Confederate States of America; you do not see me as I am, how the years have mangled me. I spit into the face of time that has transfigured me. (By the way, lass, I am very proud of that line, and I guarantee some future poet will steal it and give me no credit.) I now regulate a lottery, I snore, I suffer the gout and have spells of dropsy, I have lost most of my teeth, whereas, you, my flower, you have skin soft as a magnolia petal and as aromatic; fire blazes in your loins whereas I suffer only smoldering embers; the future beckons at your fingertips whereas my fingertips have gnarled and stiffened with age; you are ripe with potential progeny whereas soon I shall, no doubt, return to childhood myself given the brain atrophy that runs in my family; you glow with the torch of maiden zeal whereas mine own passion has dwindled into that of a dim star in the firmament; whereas, whereas, whereas—" And in this manner Beauregard would have continued except that in rehearsals of this paean to lost youth before his mirror he always burst into inconsolable sobs until enticing himself to drift back and bask in reveries of the sweet carnage of battle.

After the row with her father Miss Yunt succumbed to attacks of panic and amnesia. She would sneak out of the house at midnight disguised as a beggar, wander the streets and forget who she was or where she was going, which explains why one morning she awakened not in her familiar veiled teester bed but upon an old straw mattress in a dank oppressive room with stone walls spongy with lichen. It so happened that she had fainted on Marie Laveau's doorstep on St. Ann Street in the Vieux Carré, and the voo doo queen's attendants had carried her in. "Dem runaway make good minion," Marie laughed as the attendants tossed the unconscious girl onto the mattress and threw a horsehair blanket over her body. "I teach dis one good." She stroked the body of the serpent coiled around her neck and shoulders and chuckled. "Lil white girl from plantation, ha, time for some *black* abracadabra."

Miss Yunt opened her eyes and thought surely she had died and gone to heaven, for she beheld the most angelic face she had ever seen, a woman who were ruby lipstick and whose straw colored skin looked almost translucent. Wide golden loops dangled from her earlobes and bronze, copper, silver, platinum and gold bands, all studded with colorful gems, corseted her long, slim neck. Her dark eyes were wide, lambent and mesmerizing. A thick oily snake that smelled like almonds draped loosely from her shoulders. Miss Yunt's desire for men ceased instantly and for the rest of her life she pined only for women, though this forbidden sapphic lust never once consummated itself. She worshiped her goddesses from afar and Marie Laveau up close.

"White girl," Marie laughed, "I like men. So forgit it. I slept wit Lafayette, wit Governor Mouton and Isaac Johnson and Paul Hebert and Wickliffe and Moore and all da mayors of dis city, any man I choose or crave. And dat general who got you all hot, him too... but don't worry, his bayonet jus about daid. We gonna woik on you, git you some power yo own. By da way, I part white too. Just talk like dis for show. I could, er, discourse as primly as you debutantes at tea, but the patois seems rather anemic, pray. So les git it straight. I da queen, I own da city, you my virgin neophyte. I ain't no Zombie worshiper neither like dem Haiti's. I believe Jesus Lawd da redeemer, I prays to Virgin Mama and St. Expedite, who make miracles befo you snap a finger, I go to mass at St. Louie Cathedral, I got rosary beads in one pocket my skirt, gris gris bag in da other. I can make somebody disappear for da right price. Cure da dyin' too. We git you dress, make you look good nuff to eat like a muffin, den go to Congo Square where we gonna do some fine dancin'. Put all dem folk in a trance, git em loose, make some money."

And thus Miss Yunt commenced her journey into the supernatural underworld of black magic, hoo doo, orgiastic rituals, hexes, curses, fortune telling, Christian satanism and good old-fashioned witchcraft. She became a seasoned practitioner, altered the course of many lives, made a living and assumed her role as heir apparent until it dawned on her that such a role had been reserved for one of Marie Laveau's fifteen children, a daughter who looked exactly like her mother (but, according to some, more ruthless). She confronted Marie on the issue, and a hairline crack that soon widened into a fissure, then chasm, severed their camaraderie and friendship, an alliance Marie had nurtured despite Miss Yunt's calcified soul. Eventually Miss Yunt retired to the house bequeathed to her by her long-deceased father and attempted to practice what Marie had taught her, but Marie had put the gris gris on her in the form of a small cloth bag that contained pulverized red pepper, goofer dust from the grave of a leper in St. Louis Cemetery, a dehydrated vampire bat wing, one of General Beauregard's pubic hairs, and ground-up crocodile teeth. Miss Yunt spent years searching for the bag, with no success, in a frantic attempt to undo its effects. She had no idea that gris gris could be implanted in one's soul. Marie Laveau had not after all taught her *everything*.

Louis Gallo

Miss Yunt's fingers bled as she stabbed hatpins into two battered straw dolls that resembled Jake and Dougie, but the two neighborhood ruffians never disappeared or developed dread diseases or turned into reptiles. Hatred kept her alive, plus the little money she made selling medicinals by mail order through the tabloids. Her best sellers included Passion Powder, Victory Mist, Satan's Oil, Bad Luck Water, Man Fix lotion, Miracle Root and Ground Nutria Clay. And her best customers included Vice President Richard Nixon, Charles De Gaulle, Governor Earl K. Long, Mayor Victor Schiro, Leonid Brezhnev (through emissaries) and Frank Sinatra. Sometimes, in moments of senility, she forgot who she was and sold a potion to herself.

She had not left the house in over twenty years, but memories of previous excursions to City Park to collect Spanish moss, locust wings and snake eggs tormented her because even with averted eyes she could hardly miss the gargantuan statue of a mounted Beauregard at its entrance. She was obsessed with resurrecting the general from the dead so that she could induce a slow torturous second death through black magic. At each failed attempt she would curl into a feeble shrimp-like wisp and lullaby herself to sleep in extinct languages she had learned from Marie Laveau. In her dreams Marie's snake, named Zombi, coiled itself around her abdomen and penetrated its head into her most sanctified chapel.

The Beast in the Jungle

I escort Grandad on the torturous journey from his room to the dining room at the back of the house. I support him by wrapping my arm around his shoulders and nudging him forward inch by inch, my other hand clutching the crook of his elbow. His rheumy eyes dart about in stuporous bewilderment. He has drifted into Cloud Cuckoo Land with no return ticket.

Jenna flits about the kitchen finishing up our Thanksgiving supper. Grandad is her father, who came to live with us a few years ago when he began to fail. His room now smells like old, dusty sadness, and it's where he confines himself—meaning, for us, a regimen of bed pans, meal trays, oxygen treatments and all the onerous rest of it. He spends his time lying in bed staring at a television screen with no volume and has not spoken a word since last Thanksgiving. Our family doctor marvels that he's still alive. Down to ninety-eight pounds, this once strapping, solid bulkhead of a man.

The girls have already set out plates and utensils and glasses, and now they're off horsing around on the front porch. I aim Grandad into his chair and he lowers himself to sit stiffly erect. Instantly he clutches a utensil in each hand and starts digging at the empty plate. "Food not served yet, Grandad," I laugh. He swivels his head and gazes into my eyes, drops his lower lip, exposing a teethless, cavernous vacuole. "Ah, we forgot your dentures. Be right back, Grandad. Just sit here and everything will be ready soon."

I rush back to his room and snatch up the dentures and, at the same time, crack the front door. Emma and Chase are giggling about something on the swing. "Time to eat, girls," I say. "Come in and help your mamma carry out the food."

Jenna has outdone herself—the usual turkey and oyster stuffing, cranberry sauce, cheese-topped baked potatoes, stuffed artichokes, buttered carrots, sweet corn, an Italian spinach soufflé (the recipe handed down from my side of the family), two pies, pecan and pumpkin, cupcakes for the girls that they glazed themselves earlier this afternoon. I light the candles, turn on some soft Vivaldi for background ease and prepare to say grace, always my job and always brief, since grace embarrasses all of us. The fine bone china glistens, the starched linen tablecloth seems immune to spills, the wine glasses full of Concord grape juice look iridescent. We're ready to dig in.

Plates full, utensils swinging, the talk begins. Chase, only thirteen, says that she dreamed about the tiger man. "What tiger man?" I ask. Jenna laughs, "Oh, we saw this reality show last night while you were over at Walmart. About this freak who thinks he should have been born a tiger."

"Let me tell," Emma almost begs, "he has tattoos of stripes all over his body and fake whiskers."

"Surgically implanted," Jenna adds.

"Mom, I was going to say that. And fake teeth, fangs, but they're not fake, they're real and that was plastic surgery too. He had his eyes slanted like a cat's and changed their color with contact lenses."

"And," Chase adds, "he lowered his voice."

"Some kind of cutting of the vocal cords," Jenna says, "so he could growl and snort more like an animal."

"You should have seen him, Daddy, he didn't look human."

"What kind of doctor performs such surgery?" I ask. "I guess they'll do anything for a buck."

"He says he has the soul of a tiger."

"He's getting claws to replace his fingernails."

"Sounds more like the soul of a lunatic. How old was this guy?"

"Fifty, he said. And he's about two thirds of the way to being a complete tiger."

Grandad coughs feebly and we stop chattering at once. He has sat through it all, apparitional and gaunt, almost non-existent. His dry, purplish lips part and he clears his throat.

"Ain't fifty a bit old to become a tiger?" he says.

Our eyes bounce off each other, ricochet all over the place. I suppose we are all waiting for a cue on how to respond to the first words the man has uttered in over a year.

Chase begins to snicker, looks my way. I grin then practically spew the grape juice in my mouth across the table. Emma bends over with abrupt, belly-heaving guffaws. Jenna tries to hold it in but soon she too gasps with laughter. Now we're all choking and laughing and squealing and we can't stop.

Grandad sits motionless, eyes vacant as the windows of an empty house, though I believe that I catch a momentary, feeble smile on his face.

As for tiger man, may he roam every jungle with the finesse and ferocity of his unspeakable station.

Bayou Road

The chicken, cages of live chickens and roosters at the Indian Market on the triangle leading into Bayou Road, across from St. Rosa de Lima, its bells reverberating through the neighborhood at all hours. They make the trek often, his mother, grandmother, sister and two cousins. Bulbous black flies everywhere, rotary fans, the putrid wafts of decaying shrimp and catfish. His mother picks out the bird. A tall, emaciated black man unlatches the cage, clutches its feet, drifts toward a fifty-gallon rusty drum onto which he hooks the feet with wire loops. The knife, which seems part of his hand, deftly slices off its head. The drum is full of heads.

But this chicken lurches, snaps the wire loops. Headless, it zigzags in frenzy on a floor silted with sawdust. No one says a word. The chicken is a demon charging straight for the boy. Blood splatters out of its neck. The boy freezes as the chicken closes in, then he bolts out the screen doors, knowing he will run forever, until they find him.

The boy drops his sack of kumquats as he flees past Joe's Butcher Shop and the French bakery that always smells like anise. It was his job, to hold the kumquats and a stalk of sugar cane. But he's too scared and drops the sugar cane too, almost tripping over it into the cobble-stoned street. He stumbles, charges again, dashes into a thicket of honeysuckle, recoils, gasps, brushes himself off, then runs past the Rivoli Theater, boarded up now because of the ax murders. He's out of breath and collapses on the banquet in front of an unpainted shotgun, an old black woman gazing from her wicker rocker. "You all right, boy?" she cries in a voice thin as tissue.

Their eyes meet. "The chicken!" he screams. She spits a wad of char into the galvanized bucket beside her rocker, looks the boy over through thick cataract lenses.

"Who the chicken?" she cackles. "That be Avenging Chicken, Apocalypse Chicken, Christ Chicken, the Retribution Chicken. You got feathers in your hair."

Just then the boy hears his mother's voice call his name. He spins on his heels and speeds towards her and the family. She soothes him, takes his hand and proceeds to lead the group down the street towards their home a block or two onward.

As they pass the wizened woman's porch the boy glares smugly in her direction. He clutches him mother's fingertips tightly.

"Puck puck puckkkkkk," the old woman rasps.

Whitney

We're gathered in the big room with its hefty stone fireplace trying to keep warm. It's a long time ago. We're all young and hormonal and insufferable. Upstate New York, atop a mountain called Claymoor or something pretentious that ends in *moor*. Lots of them around, uppity mountains I call them, each pinnacled by a gargantuan fortress. Mansion is the word—this one has about fifteen bedrooms, the whole thing constructed of heavy stone dragged up from the river. Who did the dragging? Sammy says in the past they were financed and lived in by robber barons and tycoons. Sammy owns it now after his father dropped dead at forty-two.

Impressive as hell. Nobody believed Sammy's boasts back at school when we were undergrads. But it's cold and drafty and we're all constantly carrying in new logs, stoking the kindling, adding sweaters, bunched together on the three sofas arranged in a semi-circle around the flames. You can literally walk into the fireplace—it's that spacious. The old 1920s radiators in each room stay icy to the touch even when set at full blast.

We're still in college or just recently out. One of us is edging through law school now, Rick. He's here with a girlfriend he will marry in a few months. Sammy, our host, bides his time. With money you can do that. Rick used to be my best friend, way back before college, before I'd even met Sammy. We three belonged to the same fraternity, though I couldn't stand it and dropped out after the first year. It's law school that killed me and Rick. His first year and he's talking about how much power he will have.

Sammy's father sold historical calendars to the big breweries as premium giveaways. Just think up some catchy theme—like relating each day of the year to, say, a milestone in women's liberation- do a calendar, make millions. He should have known better than to fiddle with time.

Some others here too, like my current girlfriend, Rachel, who will fly home next day or so while I spend a few more days with Sammy. It's an off-on deal with some minor violence thrown in like bitter salad spices. I keep my eyes open. Then the jerk of a law professor, one of Rick's teachers, trying to stay hip with long, sandy hair, caved-in cheeks, wire glasses and endless plastic sandwich bags full of marijuana. Very good weed, though I regret giving him any credit at all. His wife, Vera, I think that's her name. Another law professor. Same stringy hair and glasses, long hair, thin sallow face. The two look like male-female clones of each other. Hands-on, hungry, sarcastic jaws working their way up the rungs. He's debating over teaching versus private practice in D.C, where he says he'll make a lot more dough.

There are others too, friends of the lawyers, but I can't remember them. No one interesting except maybe this one called Whitney, a grad student somewhere up here in the Catskills. This is not my territory. I'm deep south, tropical, in grad school myself on a fellowship. Living month to month on the paycheck. The hand I was dealt, so I don't think about it much aside from occasional spasms of envy and regret.

Sammy, always the mover, likes gathering people together. He stands back and watches the intermingling and secretly, I think, enjoys a good personality clash here and there. Or maybe he sincerely hopes to nurture us, bring us all together as some loving, happy family. He's the common denominator, a behind-the-scenes auteur. And a natural host, providing top-notch booze and food- lots of caviar, pate, deli sandwiches, egg nog, ham and turkey roasts. He drives down to the market every day for supplies. And let me tell you, the road is treacherous, what with snow blanketing the earth. It's the Christmas holidays after all. Sammy's battered old station wagon slides all over the place. The other day he wound up in a ditch with a cracked axle and had to call towers down in the valley.

The truth is there's not much to do around here. Can't get back to Manhattan, only a two-hour drive usually; can't spend much time outdoors because of below zero wind chill; can't roam the house because you'll freeze to death inside; can't watch television because Rick doesn't believe in them and there's only a tiny set in one of the bedrooms, an old ten-inch black-and- white with no reception. So we all spend a lot of time reading and trying to make small talk. The first few days or so we got into serious discussions about the big issues, clashed, learned to distrust and steer clear of each other. It's as if war were about to erupt.

The one thing we wind up doing a lot is cards, mostly poker, because, well, what else is there? I never play cards, shudder at the very idea of table "games," haven't handled a deck since I was a kid. But my old grandpa taught me a thing or two about poker. Back then I had no idea it would ever come in handy. The lawyer and his wife must have memorized Hoyle's because they know all these fancy, weird gambling games and want to show off. But the rest of us protest and finally prevail because without us, it's Solitaire, not poker. We wind up with five card draw or seven stud, easy no-brainers. The lawyers and Rick, of course, have lots of money to bet. The rest of us don't. I can't afford to lose one penny.

So I decide to make a little spare change.

The lawyer, Dave, had taken instant aversion to me and vice-versa. I don't like his snotty arrogance and wire glasses. He hates me because I don't want to bag his wife. He's one of those guys—there are lots of them around—who wants all other men to want to crave his wife. It must make them feel macho and giant-balled. He doesn't really want anyone messing with her, he just likes it when they *yearn* to. And I've made it pretty clear that I have no interest whatever. Guys can always tell when other guys are sniffing. It's all in the eyes, the joshing, the feeble compliments and enthusiasm. In effect, I'm telling Dave that his taste in women sucks. Thus he's peeved and seeks revenge.

Or maybe I'm distorting the issue altogether. I am, after all, telling the tale. Dave is long gone on one of the byroads of history, and so is his wife—though I heard later that they divorced. Maybe Dave can't even remember my name.

Mostly it's Rick, Sammy, Whitney, Dave, Trudy (his wife), this guy Mark and I shuffling the cards. Rachel and I aren't getting along. I'm feeling pretty low. We'd replaced one of sofa's end tables with a proper game table near the fire. The other guests join in every now and then, but their hearts aren't into it. Mine isn't either, but I want to make some money and I'm pretty sure I can. Anyway, the games become serious after a day or so and now often last until dawn.

Whitney makes a point of letting us know that she's one of those embittered feminists who hold men responsible for all evil. She *presents* herself as such but I can't decide if she's genuine or a party-liner. Anyway, during the games, the conversation drifts to the difference between men and women, and, bingo!, every time I say a word she jumps all over me. As if there aren't any differences! But that's exactly her position: society alone, male-dominated of course, creates the differences. Otherwise, we'd all be the same. Little does she know that I agree with her, hook, line and what's the other thing? But I'll never admit it to her, given her rigid, cold self-righteousness. Her fury. So who's worse in this confrontation?

"That's preposterous," I declare.

So we get into hormones, anatomy, the extra Y chromosome… all of it. But we're antler-locked because nobody's willing to yield an iota. Meanwhile, Dave baits me at every turn with trivia questions. He must spend his nights memorizing them for occasions such as this. Historical stuff like, What's Herbert Hoover's middle name? He thinks I'm a smart ass and wants to outsmart me. He's paying only minimal attention to the Whitney situation, though Trudy chimes in often enough on Whitney's side. Rick and Sammy won't help me out. They hardly say a word but every now and then exchange glances. I could use an ally.

The more I drink and toke the better Whitney looks, but she's fierce, hostile, poisonous. I wish she'd take off the wire rims. Blue eyes, long blond hair almost to her waist, she's wrapped in layers of wool. But there's a disconnect between the sweet Heidi look and all that rage, so I pull the switch and withdraw from the games—not the poker, just everything else that's going on. Dave keeps passing joints around and I'm feeling all right, comfortable but withdrawn. Herbert Hoover, every second word from his mouth. I just sail into a sea all my own, with special background music: *Herbert Hoover* to the tune of the Hallelujah Chorus.

I've won practically every hand. After a while, when he's lost another twenty-five bucks, Dave looks me in the eye and says flatly, "You're good."

Not good, Dave, just severe. The simple, dumb secret of poker is bluffing. Bet high and reckless and keep raising the stakes even if all you have is a pair of deuces. Keep a straight face. And never show your cards even after the game's over. Nobody can stand a straight face, and most drop out after a few rounds and you're left with one die-hard who thinks he'll clobber you with his mighty ace of spades. That die-hard is always Dave. Whitney's one of the first to fold every time. Then Trudy and the rest of them.

Maybe the simple, dumb secret of life itself is bluffing.

It's late Christmas Day and Dave, Trudy and their troupe are leaving in the morning. They're upstairs packing, making a lot of noise and endless phone calls. Rick and his fiancée have already left. So has

Rachel. Sammy's down in the valley getting more food and supplies. I'm sitting alone by the fire, about seven hundred dollars richer. But I feel a little hollow and groggy and decide to take a walk outside. Behind the house there's a gentle slope full of white birches, one of my favorite trees. Much of the snow has melted and you can trudge through the stuff without chunks of it sliding between the boots and socks. And it's a little warmer than usual.

So I'm just hiking a bit with a long branch to keep my balance. I stop a moment to take in the beauty surrounding me, breath in the cold, crisp air. From here you can't see any houses or signs of civilization or people. Kind of nice. I figure it's all over between Rachel and me finally— and that's ok too. We were lonely and sad with each other. How stupid is that?

I hear a *swoosh* from one of the white capped burning bushes and out flies the reddest cardinal I've ever seen. Crystals of snow explode into mist as the stems fall back into place and silence resumes. The cardinal disappears. Everything is white and cloudy. I'm surrounded by white birch and burning bushes. It's so peaceful and spectacular that for the first time since arriving I'm glad to be here. Delight, that's what I feel. I figure that the only people who know much delight these days are little kids.

But my toes start to freeze with numbness and I'm hungry, so I start back for the house. The wood smoke smells good. Sammy uses only hickory. Hungry too for some of that leftover ham and pineapple. Just as I ram the staff into a soft spot of ground for bearing, I'm suddenly knocked face down flat into the snow as if stuck from behind with a hundred or more pounds of dead weight. At first I think maybe it's a falling branch, but no, it's got arms and legs that clutch my body like adamant vices. I'm on the ground, spitting out snow, cursing, crying out. The arms and legs ease a bit and I manage to twist around for a glimpse of what's assailed me. Whitney! She's wearing a heavy military looking surplus jacket and thick wool cap. She just stares at me, specks of snow dotting her cheeks. For the first time I notice she has freckles.

"Jesus!" I cry. "What the hell are you doing? Were you following me?"

She doesn't say a word, just keeps staring with what I take as pure hatred. No expression on her face at all. She looks like the snow.

I wriggle loose from her body and stand up and brush myself off. She now squats on the ground gazing at me.

"What is wrong with you?" I roar. "You could have broken a bone!"

My face is scratched from scraping against some twigs as I went down. There's a little blood.

Whitney squats, saying nothing, like some animal on the hunt.

"You're crazy," I say. I snatch up my staff and thrust it back into the mud, limp away fast The fall twisted something in my left ankle. All I'm thinking as I ascend the slope is, "Hell, this is going to hurt." I spot the woodpile and Sammy's station wagon. He's back with more food. I don't even look back to check on Whitney. She can crouch out there forever for all I care.

And that's the last I saw of her. She never returned to the Sammy's, not even for her bags and luggage. For a while we thought maybe she had wandered off and frozen to death. Sammy and I searched some, then called the police. But later Dave phoned to say she'd hitched a ride with them to the airport. So at least she didn't die.

It's many years later and sometimes I still think of Whitney. Mostly she's a blur except for the freckles. I see them clearly, like tiny, scintillant specks of time. She's just some random woman I happened to encounter back in the days. I've tried to figure out why she attacked me, but every time I think I've nailed it one way or the other, I change my mind. None of the options are good. I have no idea why she attacked. She didn't lose that much money. An odd sexual game maybe, but not the kind of approach that kindled my fire. I saw no ardor or interest in her eyes. Only blank ferocity.

A few days later I too flew home to face varied strains of music and Sammy returned to the city. I left him a hundred bucks to help with the expenses, stuffed it between two books on the mantle above the fire, one of them Freud's *The Psychopathology of Everyday Life*. I don't believe anyone else left a dime of gratitude. But surely the rich have learned by now that it's better to give than receive.

Hunger

Dixie's pure Cajun out of Bayou des Allemandes where her family owns everything, oil money, but she's sweet, gracious, and makes sure her copper red hair bounces when she talks, and she's animated, lively, innocent I guess, the kind of innocent that's been around, and she laughs a lot, smiles constantly, but deep down she's sad, you can feel it, and today I bring her over to our family's Sunday feast at my grandmother's, which I don't usually do with just anyone, so for now I'm into Dixie and her eyes bulge when she beholds the food on my grandmother Meem's table because Meem goes all out when I invite guests, and back then most of my family is still alive and I will be lonely when they're not but what can you do? I'm close to Meem, real close, but I know she judges the women that come round and doesn't like any of them because I'm the crown prince according to her though she's really the boss… look at this: a platter of bruschetta dripping with butter and olive oil, the baked ham and pineapple, chickpea soup, tagliatelle pesto, artichokes stuffed with Progresso breadcrumbs and oyster paste, a bowl of fava beans with olive salad, and for dessert we'll have lemon ricotta cake and caramel flan (the best in the world)… we all dig in and Dixie eats daintily, exclaiming with each bite *how delicious* though I happen to know she prefers French to Italian, and I mean Cajun French–they eat alligators down there—and speak some twangy patois that sounds like Japanese.

But Dixie's too hungry, she's always hungry, and I like her much, how could anyone not? and she's damned fine looking and drives an MG convertible, and I don't mean by hungry greedy, there's no greed in her soul, she's just famished, and she wants to eat me up too and that might be fine if I felt like being eaten and sometimes I do but right now I don't so it's rough dealing with her and she never gets enough of, well, you know what I'm talking about, as if deprived her whole life, and I know it was a messy divorce, she crushed when her husband confessed he prefers men, which must have bludgeoned her self-esteem, and I'm sorry for her and want to help but I don't want consumption (and I don't mean tuberculosis though I don't want that either), I mean being swallowed anew each day and she can't help it, she's needy, and when I explain it to her, she cries and promises she'll change but she can't change because Dixie is Dixie and I remember times when I felt the same need and it's desperate, scary, nobody likes it, but she almost begs, pleads, she'll do anything anybody wants, just *love me, love me,* but love is a mystery and you might wind up with Medea or Medusa while eager Dixie languishes on the sidelines, still compliant, ready to forgive, and, hell, the girl is rich and hot, so why the hesitation? Oh yeah, I forgot to mention spumoni, we have that too, and get this, hand made by Meem.

We're full, bloated, but Dixie accepts a second round of flan and spumoni, and that's what I mean, how is it possible? She's not fat, she's lean and trim, and that wavy hair bounces and she's laughing and telling Cajun stories and even my half senile grandfather is charmed, charming, she's charming, though I know that after this grand lunch I'll drive her to the gazebo in Audubon Park and tell her we need to see other people (that cruel line which covers a lot of ground) and she will burst into tears and I don't want to use the word *grovel* because I really like this girl and have a few needs myself, many needs, and I wish Meem were still alive, and the others too, and Dixie's so ready to comply and enthusiastic despite the telluric sadness and it's a mistake but maybe another place, another time, because right now, at this instant, I'm hungry for nothing.

Thieves

Vera fell in love with my mug when it appeared as a TV news blurb. She confesses this as we lie in bed hugging, smooching, toking one joint after another.

"I knew I was ugly but not that ugly," I laugh. "You look like a villain," she says, squeezing me tighter, robustly. "From when you stole our chandelier from that old lady's house, right?"

Yeah, broke in with my sack of tools and found a ladder in the woman's storage closet. I carried it to the entrance hall, climbed up and systematically unscrewed the bolts connecting the chandelier to a plaster ceiling. A gem—glass crystal pendulums, maybe a hundred. Brass structure. Had to be at least two centuries old. I knew this antique dealer who would shell out for a piece like that. So there I was carrying the thing down the street when the fuzz cruised by. I tried to run but they caught me, confiscated the chandelier, arrested me on the spot.

"What about the old lady?" she asks.

"I heard she fainted when she came downstairs and found a big hole in her ceiling. Hell, I spent thirty days in jail for nothing. They found her spread-eagle on the floor, revived her, re-attached the chandelier. I'm glad to hear she's ok now. She even asked about me, said anyone who steals something beautiful deserves to have it. Imagine that."

"You're what's beautiful," she says. "I like bad boys. "Maybe you could steal something beautiful for me? It would be so romantic."

So soon enough I'm back at the old lady's house. This time I knock and when she answers I ask if I can steal her chandelier again since, as she told the cops, I deserve it. She smiles, nods and lowers herself onto a tapestried nouveau sofa.

"I got this replacement for you," I say. "High tech model from Home Depot. It has a built in converter to transform 110 volts to only 30 with the same brightness. Save you a bundle on the old utility bill." I don't tell her I stole it too right off an open Depot truck preparing to deliver it somewhere.

Once again traversing the streets with the chandelier cradled in my arms, the crystals bobbing all over the place. What a nuisance. Not exactly theft this time so I'm not worried.

I stop by my antique friend's shop and ask him what it's worth. "It's worth what somebody pays. I'll give you a hundred cash."

This means it's probably worth a grand or two since my friend is another kind of thief. So I ask myself, what's love and happiness worth? How long will it last? Say, five months max?

Vera and I lie in bed on our backs, naked, our hips almost glued together, the freaking chandelier settled atop our bodies, undulating as we breathe. She coos as she fondles each crystal, whispers she could use some silverware. Maybe a new sofa. I am so aroused I could burst.

Mama's Boy

The crumbling nunnery occupied an entire city block of Galvez Street and defined one boundary of the neighborhood, beyond which lay the *terra incognita* of moldy parchment maps, forbidden and as terrifying as the flat edge of the world feared by Portuguese mariners in the days of Prince Henry. Paw, who read a bit of history, said the nunnery proved the survival of the Dark Ages. One almost expected to see blind and crippled mendicants begging near the gates and bands of warriors watering their horses before they charged off to secure the borders of some besieged viceroy or marquis. Surrounded by soft, redolent brick, the nuns had renounced human commerce, committed themselves to the Savior's grace and sequestered themselves within His compound. During the Spanish occupation Governor Alejandro O'Reilly had imported seventeen galleons of bricks directly from Seville, bricks manufactured by artisans who belonged to a secret order of Jewish cabbalists, in order to construct the three-foot thick barrier he believed would keep the only virgins in New Orleans chaste. The nuns floated along intricate walkways, protected by parapets rising from the walls, and their silence seemed an eerie rejoinder to the earthly bustle of the neighborhood.

Jake and Dougie avoided the place because the wrinkled wraith-like sisters reminded them of Miss Yunt, a blasphemous comparison that they knew might earn them the everlasting fires of hell. Nor did they care much for the idea that nuns marry Jesus. Dougie found the notion hilarious.

"That Jeez," he laughed, "he fuckey them old ladies every night."

Jake had long suspected that Jesus had it in for him and didn't want to worsen his fate. "No," he said, "they're married but not like that." To communicate with Dougie he often resorted to his cousin's pronunciations, and he knew what the word "fuck" meant because his friend Dave Milner at McDonogh 9 had once explained it to him as a grotesque ritual during which parents become Siamese twins.

"Jesus doesn't fuckey," he insisted. "Jesus is too good."

Dougie looked perplexed. "Then what does he do?"

About ten blocks in the opposite direction the neighborhood
abruptly ceased at furious, arid Broad Street, more an ugly northern
turnpike with its constant rush of cars, buses and rumbling trucks
than the shaded lazy asphalt lanes Jake and his cousins roamed. The
neighborhood, a fragile oasis of present, seemed bounded on one side
by the unimaginable recesses of the past and on the other, a frantic,
hazardous future. In the "other" directions, *vertical* to Jake's mind,
Esplanade and LeHarpe constituted the outer, nether fringes of
reality. The cousins liked Esplanade, a sloppy wide avenue lined with
magnolias and sycamores and formidable if dilapidated mansions that
no one seemed to inhabit. Its shabby grandeur attracted little traffic.
For whatever reasons, this stretch of Esplanade never caught on, had
failed in its civic and urban potential and seemed destined to remain
a neglected bypass for stragglers and lost souls. Yet its beauty was
incontestable, unlike LeHarpe Street, which was just another street,
a little more fashionable than Columbus perhaps because the city had
paved it a few years earlier. City Hall called it progress, and the denizens
of LeHarpe therefore raised their noses slightly higher than their more
backward neighbors two streets up. But Jake and Dougie wouldn't
think of playing on LeHarp Street; along with the asphalt went the
shells, gravel and pebbles they never tired of slinging at something—
telephone poles, garbage cans, stray cats, passing cars, whatever could
be smacked, whatever made noise when smacked, whatever looked too
pristine to resist.

When they walked or rode their bikes around the corner to Galvez
Street they stayed on the side where the piano teacher lived in a house
subsumed by crepe myrtle. Jake could not understand why Miss
Gomez wanted to live across the street from a nunnery. Trudging up
her concrete steps for lessons required enough valor, although Ruthie
didn't seem to mind, probably because she played better than Jake. Jake
had perfect pitch, which she did not, but he had never learned to read
music properly because he could not stand Miss Gomez's rotten breath.
Eighth notes, he would later claim, killed him as a musician; sixteenth
notes were infernal.

Ruthie usually took her lesson first for about half an hour, after
which he and Violet would walk to Miss Gomez's house, not because
Jake couldn't find his way alone, but in order to retrieve his sister. Jake

hated the abrupt bang the teacher's screen door made when it slammed, leaving him alone in the room with her as his mother and Ruthie left for home. Through the filthy moth-clogged screen he sadly watched them fade away.

"Stop that," Miss Gomez would snarl. "You wind up a mama's boy. You want mama's boy, eh?"

The woman's breath was so vile he often felt on the verge of asphyxiation and told Dougie that Miss Gomez ate dead dogs for supper. The entire room reeked of sulfur and ammonia and the cloying fetor of human sweat laced with cloves. He would take his place next to her at the piano bench and she would say, "Now do thees arpeggio, we see how you practice." He cocked his head, but she always cupped his farther ear with her warm moist palm and nudged it upright. "Que frijo," she sighed, "put life in fingerteeps. Do arpeggio again, like Ruthie." Sometimes when she got up and hobbled to the bookcase where she kept her scores, Miss Gomez seemed to have no shape at all, that beyond looking merely old, she was more gaseous than solid and thus diffused in several places at once.

"You need new book, a more easy one," she would announce each new session as if the idea had just occurred to her. Play, Jake, por favor, the song we learn, you remember, *The Old Oaken Bucket*. As he played Miss Gomez sang along with abandon, for the tune touched her heart. Years before in Havana she had heard an American tourist whistle it as he sliced off the tip of a cigar with his Swiss army knife on the Calle Cervantes. Ruthie knew it too. They played it so often that Achille once leapt from the sofa and cried, "If I hear *The Old Oaken Bucket* one more time I'm going to rip the keys off that piano." By piano he meant the family Spinet they had pushed against one of the walls of the living room. Miss Gomez had a better piano, a baby grand, and so did Paw and Meme.

"You got no passion," the teacher sighed.

Jake assumed "passion" was a word grown-ups loved.

But he always plodded along with his lesson and actually forgot about Miss Gomez's odor whenever the music itself began to transport him. He liked to play piano. How could she say he had no passion?

When the lesson ended Jake remembered again how unhappy he always felt locked in a gloomy stinking room with a person who said *seester* for sister. Miss Gomez tried to engage in pleasant small talk but he always sped away without even telling her goodbye. Throughout the lesson he longed for the moment when his finger would separate the hook and eye on her screen door, and he would not see her for another week. A week was eternity.

Snow Story

Claire and Maddie hoped for snow, snow, snow and more snow. For Christmas they had got new snow boots and a sled, and they wanted to try them out.

Every night they asked their Mama if it would snow tomorrow.

"No snow tomorrow," Mama always said.

"But how do you know, Mama?" they whined and whimpered. "How do you know it won't snow."

"Because," Mama said, "Daddy always listens to the weather."

"How does he listen to weather?" Maddie asked. "Does Daddy have big ears?"

Mama laughed. "I mean he listens to the weather station. Some people can predict if it will snow or rain or sleet or hail or just about anything."

"I hate those people for not making it snow," Claire snorted, shaking a fist.

"They don't make the weather, "Mama said, "they only *predict* it. The weather makes itself."

"Will it snow tomorrow?" Maddie asked.

"No snow tomorrow," Mama said.

"What will happen tomorrow?" asked Claire.

"Well, believe it or not, flowers will fall from the sky tomorrow. Pretty little pink flowers."

"How do you know, Mama?" Maddie asked.

"Because Daddy told me that's what the weather station said. But sometimes they're wrong. Maybe little yellow flowers will fall instead."

At first the idea of flowers falling from the sky delighted Claire and Maddie. But then they remembered their snow boots and umbrellas and felt sad again.

"No snow tomorrow?" they wailed.

"No snow tomorrow, "Mama said.

Claire and Maddie were so distraught they began to pace the room and cry.

"It's the worse day of our lives!" Claire cried.

"It's worser than that!" Maddie corrected.

"It will never snow!" Claire moaned with sorrow.

"We'll never get to use our new shoes and umbrellas," Maddie whimpered.

"We love those shoes and umbrellas!"

"We'll just have to put them in the closet and visit them so they won't be sad!"

"Poor shoes and umbrellas!"

"It's never going to snow, Maddie."

"And we'll cry forever!"

"And all because of the stupid weather!"

"I bet some kids in other places will have snow tomorrow!"

"But we won't because we're here!"

"I wish we could move to A-las-aka!" Maddie howled.

"There's lots of snow in Alaska, Maddie!"

"But none here!"

Mama listened to them for a while, then said, "All right, you two, time to calm down. One day it will snow, I promise."

"But when, but when, Mama," the girls begged to know.

"No one knows yet," Mama said, "but it will snow. It always does. Now time for bed, monkeys. It's getting late. And you look very tired, both of you."

Deep into the night, Maddie and Claire dreamed of snow, snow, snow and more snow. It was a very good night indeed.

The next day Mama had to rouse the girls.

Rubbing sleep out of their eyes, they asked at once, "Did it snow, Mama?"

"No," but if you look out the window you'll see something strange.

The girls jumped out of bed, parted the curtains and… could hardly believe their eyes.

"Pink flowers everywhere!" they cried. "They're coming down from the sky. The whole yard is full of pink flowers!"

"Just what the weather station said," Mama laughed.

"Mama, can we go outside and play in the flowers?"

"Of course you can. What are pink flowers for if not to play in?"

Claire and Maddie dashed outdoors. They didn't need sweaters or coats or snowshoes. It was the warmest day in January on record. They waded and romped knee deep in the pink flowers and made sure to set aside two bouquets, one for Mama and one for Daddy.

"This is a great weather day!" Claire exclaimed.

"The bestist!" Maddie screeched.

"I hope it rains flowers forever!"

"This is the bestist day of our lives!"

"We love this!"

"I wish it would last forever!"

And they began to cry because they knew the best day of their lives wouldn't last forever.

"Will it snow tomorrow, Mama?" they asked right before bedtime.

"No snow tomorrow, monkeys," Mama said.

"Awwwww," the girls groaned.

"But guess what Daddy said."

"What?" they grumbled.

"Tomorrow always changes into another tomorrow."

"Oh boy, oh boy, oh boy! We love tomorrows. But what happens to today tomorrow?"

"Time to sleep, girls."

"Goodnight, Mama."

Hector Coquille

Hector Coquille had breezed in and out of Paw's childhood on his quest for the perfect remoulade. He deified Paw's mother, whom everyone called old lady Piaggia despite her married surname, as the finest and most original cook in New Orleans, and he hoped not merely to imitate but surpass her wizardry. His unabashed fawning blinded her to most of the vices which assured him routine thrashings from anonymous shadowy thugs, and he would show up disheveled and forlorn in her kitchen at any odd hour of day or night. Paw said he never saw Hector Coquille without a black eye or nasty bruise or welt. He was probably about twenty-five at the time and had acquired a sordid reputation for frequenting licentious dives in the Vieux Carre. Sometimes he hawked pastel drawings on Jackson Square or made a few dollars playing clarinet in Dixieland bands on Bourbon Street, but mostly he sold his own body in exchange for whatever money he could get, which often amounted to only a few coins since Hector was not, to his own unrelieved dismay, an even remotely attractive man. His lips were far too florid and bloated in proportion to the rest of his sullen, angular face; his cheeks had sunken into dark foggy caverns because, as he explained to old lady Piaggia who in time had become both a trusted confidante and tutor in the culinary arts, he wept bitterly every night over the endless misfortunes that beset him. Hector's waxen yellow hair arranged itself on its own accord into helical strands that resembled the snakes of Medusa and made him seem to possess far less hair than he actually had. And, alas, he looked *old*. (Rumor had it that Hector had aged an entire decade in one instant when, during his eleventh birthday party—the other children belting out a raucous "Happy Birthday to You"—he instantly discovered desire, which raced through his body like twisted barbs of voltage.) He was so petite and emaciated that a tormentor had once spat and swaggered away mumbling that beating him would be like swatting a fly. Yet despite his homeliness, Hector never really envied any other man, no matter how spartanly chiseled or cherubically beautiful, for the sole reason that nature had endowed him with the most magnificent sexual organ imaginable. He spent so much time measuring and fondling the extraordinary appendage that he had worn off the inked scale markings on his tape measure. If someone challenged his boast that the nether limb, even when flaccid, approached twenty solid inches, he instantly arranged a demonstration in exchange for a few more coins.

"It hangs down to my knees!" he would gasp, beside himself with delight. Moreover, the organ seemed indestructible as if constituted of cypress rather than human flesh. To make a little more money he would allow Paw and his friends to roll over it with the tires of their bicycles as he lay on his hip on the sidewalk, the thick, muscular shaft stretched out full length. "Hector," they would cry when in the mood, "let us roll over your weenie again!"

"How much money do you have, little boys?" Hector would snarl, glancing down at the urchins along the sizeable arch of his nose.

Hector's devotion to this remarkable facet of anatomy could hardly fail to acquire religious significance in his own mind. He loathed the word "penis" and came to call it, and all other male organs, flambeaux, after the flaming cruciform torches borne by blacks during Mardi Gras parades. "My flambeau doesn't feel well," he might sulk on gloomy overcast days, or, in better times, "My flambeau will rise above this slough of despond." He became so intoxicated with himself that he could induce trances and envision the organ as a literal flambeau, fiery at the tip and expanding brazenly above city streets and crowds of bacchic devotees. He saw flambeaux everywhere, in a direct line of vision or out of the corners of his eyes, even behind his head. "The whole world," he gushed with hungry excitement, "is a bon fire of sacred flambeaux. Flambeaux have acquired the attributes of God. I can tell you the race and creed of a person by merely glancing at the contour, plasticity, hue and magnitude of his flambeau. The Italians far exceed, say, the Egyptians to my own personal taste, yet this is not to say that Egyptian flambeaux are any less worthy of respect. Then you have your rather limpid Swiss flambeaux, the volatile flambeaux of the French, the pale Scandinavian *schlongs* (so apropos a term in their case), the Korean sausages, the English dildoes, the remarkable curvature of the Portuguese, and oh, the Semitic torque. Let us pray. Our Flambeau, that art in heaven, hallowed be Thy name."

Routine weeping aside, Hector refused to allow circumstances to defeat him entirely; to this end he adhered to a ritual of benefaction every night, expressing gratitude to the creator for the few trinkets he did in fact possess. With the methodical precision of an accountant, he appraised and caressed every object in the one greasy shoebox of a room above the Sicilian grocery where he lived, puckered his abundant lips and kissed the possessions with feverish reverence. "Thank you, my keys," he would chant while passionately kissing each key on his key ring, "for opening so many doors otherwise closed to me. Thank you, my candle," he continued, suffering burns from molten wax dripping from the flame, "for spreading, like India ink in a glass of water, this droplet of hopeful light into an overwhelming darkness. Thank you, my alligator skin billfold… my sturdy Italian boots… my precious bottle of Bay Rum (oh, how could I survive without inhaling your precious essence?)… my cracked Bavarian platter on which I have served Mrs. Piaggia's divine ravioli… my celluloid comb and hair receiver, for I too lose a little every day… my little brass lamp with its etched glass shade which I am told belonged to my Cyprian grandfather, whom alas the yellow fever ravaged before I was born… my battered Victrola which magically generates the ethereal melodies of Schubert and Verdi, without which I would summarily expire… my two books, the *Collected Works of Rabelais* and *The Unexpurgated Boccaccio*, both having taught me gaiety and tolerance…" And on it went until finally he reached the summit of his ecstasy and thanked the flambeau which had impatiently awaited the moment by becoming engorged with more and more blood. "Thank you, O Steadfast Flambeau, my Ziggurat of Ur, my Halley's Comet, Washington Monument and Proboscis of Rare Pleasure," he gasped with excitement close to delirium as he bent over and sucked the rush of fire into his mouth between moist, ravenous lips.

Paw, of course, eliminated most of the lurid details but he could not resist relating the amazing fact that he and his friends had rolled over Hector Coquille's sexual organ with their bicycles. "It was impossible," he would exclaim with dumbfounded pleasure, "the thing resisted pain and disfigurement. He just put it back in his pants and walked down the street!"

Old Lady Piaggia knew nothing about the antics of her son, and Hector was wise enough to keep his own more unsavory adventures to himself. She looked upon him as a lost soul and as such he stirred her compassion, much as she stirred the omnipresent cauldrons of tomato sauce always simmering on the burners of her stove.

"But what do you add to give the sauce that almost Mephistophelian flavor?" he begged to know.

"Hector," the old woman replied, "it's only thyme, garlic, parsley and salt. I don't know what flavor you mean. Wait, I add a little marjoram. Maybe that's it."

So Hector would rush to the French market and buy a handful of freshly picked marjoram to add to his own kettle. But it was never quite right, always flat and unmemorable, unlike the druidic creations of his mentor, and he despaired of discussing proportions with an old lady who cooked by instinct, not science. "And what about that linguini? It looks as if you scoop it out of the colander and simply plop it on a plate, wet and glistening, like a heap of pale worms. But then, again, that taste. What could it be? It's not the cheese, though the Romano certainly participates. I think it's sweet basil this time. But how remarkable… the sauce looks invisible! I love the deception. When that mysterious flavor seduces my tongue, I could stuff myself like those gluttonous Roman senators whose stomachs exploded at their own banquets."

But Hector's mission remained above all to master the occult properties of the perfect remoulade. "Most are either nasty old ketchup or some viscous cream sauce. Forget the creams, they are defilements which rarely compliment the shrimp. If there's one thing I can't stand it's white remoulade. No, it's got to be red… and, of course, spiked with tabasco. But the secret I believe lies in the horseradish. A remoulade without horseradish is a crime against nature. But how do you grind it properly? How long can you wait before mixing the ingredients? Should the horseradish cause pain or be more subtle?"

Old lady Piaggia could not help Hector with remoulade because she dismissed it as a Gallic abomination. She excelled at only Italian food, and north Italian at that. "The Sicilians and Sardinians have simple, callous tongues," she reminded her student. "They are like those blacks who always choose the brightest, boldest colors for their attire. I am from Genoa myself, and the Genoese rely upon scent before taste. So the trick is to subdue flavor with the help of your nostrils until it releases itself on the palate. This is what you miss, Hector, you're too impetuous."

Invariably Hector would sob and swear to her that he would hang himself from a live oak in Audubon Park before nightfall because at this rate he would die anyway—before discovering the hermetic properties of an immaculate remoulade, the sauce, he wailed, of Plotinus and Moses de Leon.

"There, there," the old lady consoled, "you shouldn't kill yourself over remoulade. What do the French know? They were still barbarians when Marcus Aurelius composed his memoirs and refined the tenets of Stoicism. Or when Diocletian, that humble Illyrian peasant, separated east and west. Stop that whimpering. And what's this I hear about your carousing on Decatur Street at three in the morning? What could possibly keep one awake at three in the morning?"

Hector would then launch into another intricate, contrite confession to himself and promise to reform before Greek mariners at the Acropolis Bar bludgeoned him with crowbars in some dark alley. But such a death was so unthinkable he soon returned, with the instinct of a homing pigeon, to the origin of his misery, the unattainable remoulade of his dreams and appetite. "Do you think sage might work? I've heard that North American Indians used it to purify both themselves and their possessions because they believed it contained benevolent spirits. I want my remoulade to exude spirituality so that people who taste it will experience religious mortification, then redemption."

"No," old lady Piaggia would grunt as she began to slice the one cow brain that she added to her ravioli filling to achieve consistency, destroying Hector once again, "sage is too harsh. It would be like adding alum to the most delicate meringue." Her reprimand smote him like the broadside of a cutlass; frustrated beyond consolation, he skulked away into the night to seek out the most depraved joint in the Quarter. He burst through the door like a rambunctious cowpoke, unzipped his pants, clutched the flambeau at its base and swung it around like a lariat. "Hello, everybody!" he cried as his hips slowly gyrated, and the lariat, because of its neutronic density, began to engrave glowing afterimages of its own parabolas into the nearly opaque smoke saturated air.

Columbus Street

Every consciousness mutation is apparently a sudden and acute manifestation of [the] latent possibilities of present origin.
—Gebser, *The Ever-Present Origin*

There's old Chin slouched on the concrete steps plucking water chestnuts out of a can. Chin the Chink. They say he came to America as a stowaway during World War II. He's about a hundred years old and so skinny his legs have dwindled into two pieces of wire. His khaki pants lie flat on the steps as he eats the chestnuts from Hong Kong Emporium on Decatur Street. They're poisonous, dad says. Only chinks can eat them because they're immune. Dad says Chin catches the bus on North Miro, rides up to Esplanade, then transfers all the way to the Quarter. The bus lets him off on Royal Street and he walks over to Decatur. We wonder how he manages on two pieces of wire. We think maybe he floats. He's about the most silent old man we've ever known. He just sits on the steps slurping those chestnuts. And licorice. Long strings of slimy licorice that look like black spaghetti. Old man Piaggio across the street says the licorice cured him of leprosy. There's a bowl of sardines beside Chin's loafers for Quinine, one of the neighborhood cats, a bloated, orange and white tom with one ear missing. Tomorrow we will find him flattened by a car in the middle of the street. He daintily nibbles at the sardines next to Chin's shoes. We don't know what smells worse, the shoes or the sardines.

Dad says Chin lost his mind when a rat bit him on the ship to America. No doctor would treat him because he was in stowaway, so the rat disease spread through his bloodstream into the brain. We move toward the steps and whisper, old Chin, old Chin, old Chin, old Chin. His eyes don't even blink. But every now and then he'll stretch his purple lips from one end of his face to the other in a contorted grin and say, *Jean et Philippe etudiant,* or something foreign like that. Then he holds a long strand of licorice above his head by the tip and lets it coil into his mouth. It smears his lips and face black and makes him look like a rotting corpse.

We're glad we don't have to get up early because that's when Peg-Leg roams the neighborhood. *Clomp clomp clomp* goes the peg, Dad says, a noise we never want to hear.

The little girl on the porch comes later. Her parents moved into the house after Chin died or left the neighborhood, though we kids think he got skinnier and skinnier until he just dissolved. The house isn't much to speak of, half a house really, like most of the houses on Columbus Street. Shotguns. Our family lives in the right side of the shotgun, Chin and the rest of them in the left. We have three main rooms plus a bath in the middle and a kitchen to the rear. The kitchen window roars with a gigantic, box-like window fan. When it's hot, Dad puts a block of ice on a shelf behind the blades and you can feel the sweat on your face freeze. There's always a yard where generations of animals have been buried. And dusty, stunted banana trees. Sometimes a red pepper bush with peppers so hot their juices can blind you. This happened to Mr. Larry down the street. He picked a red pepper, then rubbed the sleep out of his eyes. The acids corroded his corneas and now he stares into space with eyes that look like the whites of fried eggs. The yards are bounded by high wooden fences that have lost their paint. The boards are gray and soggy like sponge, though we kids still manage to climb them. Sometimes we clutch a piece of soft, rotten wood and come crashing down, and out mothers shout, be careful. So we're careful for a while and then start climbing again.

The little girl has blond hair and a twisted left foot. She skips rope on the porch as Chin fiddles with and inspects his water chestnuts and licorice. A fat woman rocks on the swing and fans herself with a battered Esso fold-out map. It's always hot on Columbus Street. The blocks of ice behind the fan help a little. One time the rag man came around with his horse-drawn cart and the horse dropped dead of a heat stroke. Foam bubbled on its bluish lips. The rag man, black as grandma's stovepipe, wiped the sweat off his brow with his shirt and shook his head. Ain't it some shame, he mumbled. The rear end of his cart shot up vertically in the air and all the rags and bottles he'd collected scattered everywhere. The little girl sings, *One two, buckle my shoe,* as she skips rope, *Three, four, knock at the door.* The fat woman is her aunt or something. No one knows what happened to the girl's mother, but the adults whisper about it. We saw the mother once. Her blond hair swooshed around her face like a cloud of light. She was arguing with her drunk and unshaven husband. The bottom half of his face looked rusted. A Checker taxi pulled up and she rushed for it. No one ever saw her again. We call the man her father but we don't know for sure. He sits on the swing with the fat woman. He wears ribbed undershirts and rolls Target tobacco cigarettes. Our dad smokes Target tobacco too and he rolls better cigarettes. The little girl's father's cigarettes look like mangled white worms. Thank God I got my Rosie, he says to the fat woman. She waves the smoke away. She's just a doll, he says. Too bad her foot curled like that, but no curled foot's gonna keep the boys away. I just hope I live to see her get married, the fat woman sighs. Her lower arms ripple with blubber. Her flowered sack of a dress is drenched with sweat. You call somebody about those bats? she asks. The man shakes his head. Just ain't had time, Lo, he says.

We kids hope he never calls. We like the bats. They live in the giant palm tree towering over the house. Dad says it's half dead. It has no branches at all and only a clump of fronds poke out at the top, where the bats live. At twilight they swarm and make creepy squeaking noises. They're blind like Mr. Piaggio and emit radio waves so they don't smash into buildings and kill themselves. They don't exactly fly, they sort of ricochet about in awkward circles. They're after mosquitoes and bugs, which is good, because sometimes the mosquitoes are so thick they turn the air sooty. And big—big as billiard balls. Once we slapped one on the back of Jackie's neck and blood splattered all over our faces. MaMaw says it was a vampire mosquito that would have sucked out Jackie's blood if we hadn't crushed it. At twilight we bring out our flashlights and fly-swatters and go hunting mosquitoes. We put the dead ones in PaPaw's old wooden cigar boxes. One night we filled fifteen cigar boxes. We thought that would help save the neighborhood, keep some people alive. But the next night the mosquitoes were back and nobody had died, and squashing them got boring. Mom sprays us with 6-12 whenever we go outside so we won't get the sleeping sickness. PaPaw says when he was a boy they brought the yellow fever, Bronze John, he calls it. Dad says it was rats. He says they rolled wooden carts through the streets picking up dead bodies, house after house.

Clomp clomp clomp

That's around the time the Mafia came looking for PaPaw's older brother, and they would have stabbed PaPaw too—that's what they did then, they stabbed you right in the heart—except he begged this black nanny lady to let him hide under her petticoats. Those Mafia guys paced the sidewalk looking for PaPaw and his brother. The brother,

Vincent, was already dead, and later some tramps found him drowned in Bayou St. John, his feet embedded in coffee cans full of concrete. PaPaw died in 1974 of senility. He says he still can't remember what happens from one minute to the next. So we have to keep an eye on him. He sneaks out of the house and wanders around the neighborhood in his underwear. Once Miz Cleezio brought him back and he was stark naked. Nasty old man, she says.

The mosquitoes breed in the swamps and lagoons by the trillions, then fly in and spread the sleeping sickness. This is before the city sent trucks into the streets that sprayed thick, foul gasses to kill insects. Mom says the gas causes birth defects in a lot of children. If you see someone with little flaps for arms, she says, you know they breathed that gas. We don't want to see anyone with little flaps for arms. We have nightmares about those little flaps.

Five six, pick up sticks. Seven eight, lay them straight.

Sometime we go around the corner to see if Pinhead's out on his porch. He can't stand up so his mom and dad carry him out to the swing and let him sit there for hours. He makes horrible sounds, like squawks, and his head tapers up to a point. You can see the point really well because they shave his hair in a crewcut. He wears thick rimless glasses so he can read Joe Palooka comic books, which is about all he ever does. PaPaw says he's more animal than human. One time PaPaw saw him lunge off the swing and drag himself over to a bowl of dog food. He sucked it up, swinging his head back wildly and licking his lips with every bite. PaPaw makes jokes about it but Pinhead scares us kids. Like the ones with polio in the special class at McDonogh Nine school. Mom says it's polio only if they can't move at all; it's something else if they jerk around and make seal noises. Muscular disturbance or palsy, she says. She worries it's catchy and we'll pick it up if we breath the air around their special room. So we hold our breaths when we pass to get to our classes. Once every year the school has a Mardi Gras parade and the cripples get to ride their wooden wheel chairs in a circle around the cafeteria and throw beads to the normal kids. The teachers pick certain kids to push the chairs. When we get picked, we cringe. We push the chairs with our fingertips and think about nothing else but getting to the bathroom and washing our hands. It's pretty pitiful because the cripples can't really throw the beads and trinkets. They just slip out of their hands onto the floor. Most of the kids scramble for the trinkets, but we can't understand why they would want contact with anything the cripples have touched. So many germs, Mom says. At night she scrubs us down with Dr. Tichenor's Antiseptic and rubs Vick's into our nostrils. PaPaw tells her to use Zemo Ointment.

They tore that school down a while back, but kids still march in every morning for class. It went from Kindergarten to fifth. There's about a million McDonogh schools in the city, named after this old miser John McDonogh who left all his secret money to build schools. Sometimes Mr. McDonogh visits the schools. *McDonogh unto thee we rear, a monument of lasting wealth.* Maybe it's *joy*, not *wealth*. Everybody says something different, but that's the song we have to sing on school holidays. He's hunched over, bald and has a bulbous cauliflower nose. He never smiles and munches his lips the way old people do. He just prowls the halls and sometimes looks into a classroom. Our teacher, Miz Swander, waves to him, but it's a fake wave. She wishes he would go back to the tomb or something. He makes her nervous and her armpits sweat and drench her sleeves. Miz Swander smells like ashes. She eats egg salad sandwiches every day. She calls them sammiches and tells us we should eat them too because eggs are very good for you. You don't need to eat anything but eggs, she says. Miz Swander knows someone who eats the grass in her back yard. She never mows the grass because she eats it instead, on her hands and knees grazing like a cow. Sometimes she licks the stalks of sugar cane and bamboo that shoot up from a broken sewer pipe in her yard. We would like to see that, we tell Miz Swander, but she laughs. Honey, it's too sad, she says. And it's my aunt Lucille. I won't embarrass her. She's not cuckoo or anything, she just likes the way grass tastes. She works at Charity Hospital emptying bedpans and changing bandages. She might lose her job if they find out.

She's the one who told me about your PaPaw, the time he liked to hemorrhage to death after he had a hernia operation. He was still a really young man when his mamma found him bleeding in the alley and she started to scream. Dr. Johnny came running over and gave him a shot in one of his veins. Dr. Johnny said it was coffee in that shot. I didn't ask him what brand but I happen to know he likes Community Coffee with chicory. It's what saved your PaPaw's life that time, Miz Swander said. The coffee got his heart beating again. It perked him up long enough to get him to Charity in an ambulance. Lucille told me. She changed your PaPaw's bedpan. One time he got so nauseated he ran to the bathroom and threw up a big green tapeworm right on the shower stall floor. Lucille cleaned it up. She said the tapeworm was seven inches long and fuzzy. That's what ailed him, she said.

I don't like it when Dr. Johnny tries to kiss my mom. Whenever we get sick and he comes over with his black bag full of medicine and instruments, my sister and I catch him trying to kiss her. She always smiles and pulls away, saying softly, Stop it, Johnny, it's not right. But he always comes back and Ruthie and I decide it's better not to think about it. We never tell Dad, and I bet Mom doesn't either. I don't think Dr. Johnny likes our dad. Whenever they talk, Dr. Johnny smirks and yawns a lot and tries to get away as soon as he can. But Dad loves Dr. Johnny. He wants to talk to him about everything all the time. He likes to talk about short wave radio and history and geography. That's Dad. He can talk forever. Sometimes he talks to trees and the fence and even his black pickup truck. He talks to old Chin for hours at a time, or what seems like hours; when you're a kid one minute can seem like hours.

Chin just sits on the steps and swallows another water chestnut. And the little girl Rosie skips rope on the pavement. *Nine ten, the big fat hen.* The rag man passes with his cart, crying, *rags, paper, bottles.* And sometimes you can hear Pinhead squawking around the corner. He didn't live long. He died last year. But we still hear him, and when we ride bikes past his house, there he is on hands and knees, gobbling down the wet, ugly dog food. We shouldn't stare at Pinhead but can't stop ourselves. Mom says whatever's wrong with him is much worse than polio. We kids think maybe a mosquito bit him.

Peg-Leg clomps through the neighborhood every morning. Dad says he's a ghost.

We don't like Miz Cleezio much because whenever she visits MaMaw she sits at the kitchen table and giggles so much that she pees on herself and it drips and puddles on the linoleum floor. The window fan roars and drowns out our voices. MaMaw curses after she leaves and cleans up the mess. She says Miz Cleezio is feeble-minded. Miz Cleezio died of stomach cancer in 1958, but sometimes she still finds PaPaw roaming the neighborhood and guides him back to us. So MaMaw invites her over for tea and lady fingers and she pees again. She stuffs the lady fingers into her mouth until her cheeks bulge and when she talks, crumbs spray everywhere. The fan roars, the little girl sings, *eleven twelve,* the fat lady lugs the father's body up concrete steps. We don't know if he's drunk or dead. The fat lady takes care of Rosie now, but she's grouchy and always complains that it's not her child, why should she do all the work? Old Chin howls like a mad man when he runs out of water chestnuts. Sometimes our mom picks them up for him at the Hong Kong Emporium. It's right next to Central Grocery where she goes to buy Romano cheese and ravioli shells. The smells of Central Grocery almost make you faint: anise, salami, garlic, mint, coffee beans, cheeses, rotting bananas—all mixed together. The aromas saturate our clothes and skin, and we all smell like the grocery for days. Mom buys the ingredients for ravioli, but PaPaw rolls out the meat and cow brains and tomato sauce and cheese into a big slop on the kitchen table and stuffs the pasta shells. He says the cow brains are for texture. We kids don't think about the cow brains when we eat ravioli. It's a big treat, twice a year, at Thanksgiving and Christmas. It's delicious, but if we thought about the brains, we wouldn't eat it. Once we made old Chin try to eat one and he smelled it for about an hour. He put it in his mouth, chewed, swallowed and then vomited. No one cleaned up the vomit, and soon the ants crawled all over it. MaMaw says ants save us from rats and possums that also like to eat vomit. She says Chin should climb back into his grave. And that poor little girl, she says, now that she's got no father or mother. The fat lady just sits on the back steps drinking glasses of baking soda and water. She belches and retches and sometimes spits up in the galvanized pail beside her. Dad says she has dyspepsia. She lets Rosie run around with no clothes on. Rosie rolls around in the dirt in the back yard like a filthy animal. That's what the fat lady calls her, filthy animal. She says nobody will marry her now. That's when Rosie started bleeding from the hands and biting people. Some people had to come and take her away. Mom says they put her in a home for orphans. But she still skips rope as if nothing happened. *Thirteen, fourteen, maids are courting.* We kids think maybe Pinhead will marry her. Secretly, some of us would like to marry her, even with the twisted foot. Her face looks like a valentine when it's clean, and her hair, like glowing fresh straw. Sometimes grown men stare at her and fall to their knees. PaPaw says maybe she's one of those girl saints who become angels.

They come in a special white limousine to take Rosie away, just when the bats in our palm tree streak down to attack PaPaw's hair. He swats at them with his folded newspaper, rips out the claws from his head and collapses on the porch. We're in the back yard, burying Dickie, our parakeet, but we hear PaPaw screaming. There's only one bat left when we get there, and PaPaw tries to choke it to death as it hisses and screeches. His head is bloody and scratched and he worries about rabies. The bats chewed off all of his hair and it never grows back. Now he wears a black beret and sits on the porch swing and shoots the bats one by one with a b-b rifle. He's killed about five, but mostly the b-b's only stun them, they drop out of the tree, then fly back up. If they are still wriggling on the banquet, PaPaw drops a brick on them, scoops them up with a shovel and hurls them into the garbage cans up front. Every time PaPaw kills a bat the mosquitoes regroup and attack us. MaMaw fusses and screams at him to stop shooting the bats but he won't listen. *They took my hair*, he growls. Old Chin laughs because he's never had any hair since the day he was born. The rag man curses because the mosquitoes make his horse sick, and by evening we kids are swollen with itchy welts. Mom slathers on the Dr. Tichenor's but we scratch and scratch. MaMaw swats our hands when we scratch. She says we'll get red streaks from blood poison and when the red streaks reach our hearts, we'll die. Sidney Roveri around the block had a red streak that inched up from his wrist to his elbow. Every hour he marked the spot where the streak ended with a ball point pen to see how fast it was moving. When it reached his shoulder, they took him to Charity. We don't know what they do to him, but he comes back white as an onion and stays that way. And a chunk of his arm is missing. Then the city sprays gas to kill the mosquitoes and MaMaw stops fussing at PaPaw for shooting bats.

Dad's the one who wakes up before everyone, early in the morning when fog from the river rolls through the streets like clouds of bundled laundry. He teases us with stories about Peg-Leg, the old pirate who once sailed with Jean Lafitte. Peg-Leg wears a long, tattered, gray coat and wraps a faded red bandana around his head. A golden loop made by the Spanish conquistadors dangles from his left ear, and he has a black patch over one eye. A cannon ball took one of his legs, so he made himself a new leg from a cypress branch and attached it to his stump with strips of rag and rope. Dad says you hear him coming before you see him. *Clomp clomp clomp.* Peg-Leg has a girlfriend in the neighborhood and Dad says he still loves her and is trying to find her. When he was younger, he docked his ship at a Mississippi wharf and rode his horse right off the gangplank to the neighborhood. Now he's old and can't ride horses anymore, especially with the stick leg. So he takes his time.

We don't want to believe Dad and punch him on the arm whenever he talks about Peg-Leg. He tells us to get up early with him and he'll prove it. He even promises to take a picture of him with his Leica. We don't like to get up early when there's still fog, but mostly we're worried Dad is right. He always calls us chickens, so one of us finally works up the courage to get up early and hide with him in the azalea bush up front. The rest of us stay inside, though on that morning, we're far from asleep as we lie in our beds waiting to hear about what happens. It's so early dew coats the grass and leaves of the azalea bush. It's too early for Chin to be sitting on the steps. Too early for the little girl Rosie to skip rope. Too early for the rag man to come round. So Dad and one of us squeeze into the giant bush, Dad with the Leica hanging from his neck, and we wait and wait and wait in the fog. It's damp and a little chilly and squatting is uncomfortable.

The boy who isn't afraid gets tired and wants to go back to bed. Just a little longer, Dad says, pressing a finger across his lips. If he thinks we're here, he won't come. And right then we think we hear something in the distance, like when MaMaw pokes her broom handle on the back yard bricks. A faint clomp. Then louder, *clomp clomp clomp*, louder and more ominous with every step. All at once the boy beholds the breath-taking sight of Peg-Leg emerging out of the fog, limping down the sidewalk right in front of our house. He looks exactly the way Dad described him. The boy trembles, feels his blood turn to ice, and he wants to dash away, run forever. But Dad wraps an arm around him and forces him down. Shhhh, he whispers. And now Peg-Leg passes directly before the bush, so close we can reach out and touch his wooden leg. We feel his putrid, fire breath on our necks. It smells like seaweed, rotten fish, ocean salt. Dad won't release his grip on the boy until Peg-Leg takes a few more steps down the street and begins to recede into the fog again. He rises from the bush, focuses his Leica and snaps a picture. Peg-Leg hears the shutter click and slowly turns to inspect us. The boy won't look. Dad says later that Peg-Leg fixed his good eye on him and it burned. He opens his shirt and shows us the bruised-looking scar near his shoulder blade. But I got the shot, he laughs. Now they'll believe me.

At the turn of the century, a boy—the one who wasn't afraid—crawls on his knees through a dusty attic laced with oily cobwebs. He roots through a box of musty papers stored in his sweltering attic and comes across the faded black and white photograph of Peg-Leg. His heart goes wild. Dad, who died in 1986, climbs the attic stairs to join him. I told them he was real, Dad says. We gaze at the picture together. You don't see Peg-Leg's face, just a full-length shot as he hobbles away from the camera. But the wooden leg is unmistakable, and the bandana and ear ring. It seems to the boy, now a man fast approaching the age of his father when he died, that, despite the evidence, despite the photograph, Peg-Leg could not have existed, was merely one of the stories his father told. And Chin too and the bats and Rosie and maybe the entire preposterous neighborhood. His father looks sad. Why would you think that? he asks.

The boy too wonders why such a thought would have occurred to him to him. He… we, know the neighborhood is real. Pinhead still rocks on his swing, bobbing his head up and down like a broken piston. Quinine finishes off the putrid sardines. There's Rosie skipping rope again, her leg still twisted. She starts over. *One two, buckle my shoe.* PaPaw shoots another bat. The city has not yet sent trucks in to spray the mosquitoes, so MaMaw tells him to stop. We'll all get the sleeping sickness, she growls. Rosie's drunken father lies flat on his back on the pavement. The fat woman drags him up the steps. She swallows a glass full of bubbling baking soda and water. We laugh when we hear her belch and make belching noises ourselves. Brats, she mumbles. Old Chin has died. Dr Johnny tries to kiss our mother, and she pushes him away, but she smiles too. Why does she smile? PaPaw and MaMaw have also died. MaMaw tells Miz Cleezio that she can't come over anymore unless she stops peeing on the floor because guess who has to clean it up. Our parakeet Dickey flies into the window fan and all that's left of him is a few yellow feather floating in the air. We're crying as we bury one of the feathers in the back yard next to Quinine's grave. There must be a million animals buried in the back yard. Mr. Piaggio roots in the gutters for pennies and bottle caps. This is before the red pepper juice blinds him. Miz Swander tells us to eat egg salad sandwiches. She shoos Mr. McDonogh out of the classroom. Time to sing, she laughs. "O Come All Ye Faithful," since it's near Christmas time.

We want new bikes, a basketball, new baseball bats, dolls, teddy bears, a stick horse. One of us wants a camera, a real camera, like Dad's, because, he says, you never know who won't believe you. Still exploring the attic on the eve of the millennium, he begins to suspect that time has played an enormous trick on everyone. He and his mother and sister are the only ones left now, the sole survivors of the past, of a neighborhood that once flourished briefly, on Columbus Street. It seems that the intervening years, not the neighborhood, are what's illusory. This other time, this new era, is alien and uncomfortable, a shoe size too small. But still Miz Cleezio giggles and pees and MaMaw curses as she wipes it up with a rag. PaPaw is missing again. They'll find him two or three blocks away and bring him back. They took my hair, he fumes. And one of us listens for Peg-Leg with Dad. Peg-Leg, the man in the attic realizes, is Death, not the people dying one by one, Pin-Head, Mr. Piaggio, PaPaw's brother and all the rest, not single, feeble deaths, obituaries, but something broader, more majestic, winding though the streets like an endless strand of foggy licorice that you can eat. It may poison you, and they'll rush you to Charity in bustling panic because the red streak inches toward your heart; you'll come back white as an onion with a chunk of flesh missing… but you'll come back. Or maybe you won't.

The little boy who gets a camera for Christmas tells Chin to smile and say "cheese." At the bottom of the picture you see only the top of Quinine's head, that one ear stretched back as if he's attuned to some faraway sound, something we can't hear. Chin's face is smeared with saliva and licorice, and bloodied water chestnuts fall out of his mouth like the Eucharist. Just as the boy presses the shutter, he finds another dusty old photograph in the box, the one he took. But it's blank, now the color of parchment and, he remembers, the color of the sky that particular morning. The emulsion has cracked into a spidery web of veins and flakes off the paper. Chin smiles and says something foreign. *Fromage.* PaPaw shoots himself in the toe and howls. We never see Peg-Leg again, or hear the clomp, because, Dad says, he found his girlfriend and she knows voo doo and makes him young again. The man in the attic throws back his head and a cobweb enmeshes his face. I'd like some of that voo doo, he laughs, spitting out soft knots of gossamer. And because you never know who'll believe you, he stretches out his arms and aims the camera at his own

Shrine

The boy and his parents sat on the steps of their front porch watching fireflies rise from the grass like tiny holes in darkness. It had been a hot humid day, but the night coming on was sweet, full of mimosas and mountain gusts tinged with ice. An approaching storm made the family feel vivacious and alert. No three people could have been more content. Flashes of heat lightning ignited the entire sky and pugnacious gusts raked the sturdy young elm growing beside the front window as the boy sat playing with an old battered puppet and pointing to the fireflies. He was sleepy, but his parents wanted him with them for a little while longer to savor the evening.

Suddenly, voices from across the street broke the family's bubble of lazy enchantment. They could make out two people walking past the house, each holding something that glowed green, sticks or batons. When they waved the father thought he recognized one of them.

"Hallooo, Kurt," he called. It was too dark to recognize faces, but the stranger bore himself like Kurt with his lanky, awkward gait. Kurt approached other people as if he were attacking them, although no gentler soul could be imagined.

"Hey," the man replied, edging toward the curb, watching for cars. Then he and his companion crossed over, lumbered up the steep stone steps and approached the porch. It was indeed Kurt, with Sondra, which surprised the father a little, considering the hour. He almost asked, "Where's Rennie?" but checked himself. Rennie was Kurt's wife. Both Kurt and Sondra taught at the college in different departments. The father suspected nothing illicit—Kurt was famous for wandering about in a daze and showing up at odd places and times—nor could he imagine Sondra, who had acquired a "reputation," attracted to genderless Kurt. He wondered why the thought of intrigue had even remotely crossed his mind.

Kurt and Sondra had concealed the strange glowing things behind their backs, apparently planning to surprise the family.

"Look what we've got!" Kurt abruptly cried. At once they whipped forth the luminous sticks. "Boo!"

The last thing Kurt would have intended was terrifying anyone, the mother would say later, but the boy did shriek and shimmied on his behind to a dark corner of the porch where he huddled. Both the father and mother rushed after him, thinking an insect or even the dog had bitten him.

"I guess the stick scared him," Kurt called defensively. "I'm sorry. We found them in the street. Somebody threw them out of a car while we were walking."

The boy allowed himself to be consoled but could not stop shuddering. The mother smiled goodbyes and led him inside with the intention of putting him to bed She was not angry, only bewildered. Moments before she had felt a rare ease; her ceaseless worries had briefly subsided and she had allowed herself the luxury of repose. Now she scolded herself: if only she'd paid more attention she would not be scurrying her child off to bed in such a state.

"Kids, you never know," said the father, worried about his son but feeling obliged to prattle for a while. "Let me see that thing," he said, flicking his cigarette onto the lawn.

Kurt passed the stick to him. "You can have it. We've got two. I want to take one home to Scottie."

The stick turned out to be a plastic tube filled with green liquid that emitted light. Its ends were sealed, and the tube was flexible enough to bend when waved. He realized you could buy such things at Walmart and such places—"glow sticks—but he'd never examined one close up. As they talked his gaze remained upon the liquid flowing from one side of the tube to the other. Each wave made a different formation, and when shaken the liquid became a hive of tiny bubbles. The light was not intense, but it coated their faces with an eerie patina. At one point the father looked up to see Kurt and Sondra glaring at him, their faces grotesque caricatures of shadow and phosphorescence.

"It's some sort of chemical reaction," Sondra said. "You hit it on something and it starts glowing."

"I love it," said the father. "I've got to have it."

"I already gave it to you," Kurt laughed.

"Oh, come on, I can't take this. You found it."

"I insist," said Kurt. "I've got this other one for Scottie."

Socttie was Kurt's son, an angelic blond-haired boy three years younger than the father's child. Scottie was adorable, everyone agreed, but when talk at faculty parties turned to him the father felt uncomfortable and went to refill his glass or comb his hair.

"I'm really sorry we scared him," Kurt said. "We're on a hike and have to get going. Do you think we ought to stay?"

"Nahhh," the father waved. "He'll be ok. Too sleepy maybe. It was such a great night we let him stay up late."

The father, now leaning against a porch post, did want to get inside to check on his son. He fretted over him too much. The boy seemed frail and jittery. He liked music and books rather than sports, which did not bother the father, who also liked music and books, but he knew from experience that boys who played baseball and the rest of it seemed less vulnerable than those who did not. And he felt guilty that he had never attempted to teach his son how to throw a ball much less catch one.

The friends shook hands and the father went inside, locking the door behind him. He noted one last firefly floating near the top of the massive oak tree across the street. The night now seemed too dark.

He found his wife on the sofa in a dark living room staring at the television with the volume turned to mute. An old black and white movie was on. He knew the movie and suddenly realized all of its stars were dead. He made a point of turning on one of the standing lamps.

"How is he?" he asked, sinking into a battered old armchair that had belonged to his grandmother. He remembered her reading stories to him in the chair when he was hardly more than four or five years old. He remembered how the light congealed in her silver hair, her soft voice, the bulging veins in her twig-like arms that both fascinated and terrified him.

His wife had put her finger across her lips. "I'm listening to see if he's fallen asleep."

They listened together for a while and heard no rustlings no calls. The boy usually fell asleep instantly.

"What happened?"

"That damned stick you've got in your hand," she said. "It scared him."

The father looked at the tube, watched the wave inside flow from end to end.

"But why? This thing is harmless. Kids play with them."

"Well, he doesn't," she said, not accusingly but with some exasperation that the toy—they assumed it was a toy—had ever materialized.

"Kurt said somebody threw it from a car," the father said meekly.

That night the mother awoke from deep sleep with a start. She sensed someone else in the house was also awake. She squinted at the father as she groped for her glasses on the night stand. He snored and seemed profoundly unconscious. She pulled on her satin robe and tiptoed down the stairs, calling softly to her son. Her robe whisked loudly as she descended.

She found him in the front foyer sitting cross-legged and erectly on the floor staring at the green stick as it lay on the table where the father had left it. Without thinking he had set it down as he followed his wife up to bed. It would not have occurred to him to throw it away. It flashed through the mother's mind that she would have thrown it away, although she too had forgotten about it. The boy had an unusual glaze in his eyes and at first she believed he was still asleep, but he had never walked in his sleep before so it seemed unlikely. He was probably in a kind of trance, she assumed with some alarm when he did not respond to his name. He seemed entirely transfixed by the glowing green tube as if it were an object of reverence. Yet he did not protest or fight her when she pulled him up and led him back up the stairs to bed. He merely whimpered a little as she tucked him in. She inhaled the fresh starched smell of newly washed sheets and felt relieved, although the strange new stiffness of her son's body puzzled her. He felt unnaturally rigid and slightly too cool to the touch. The mother had had her frights in the past, when the boy came down with scarlet fever or ear infections, so she allowed her maternal instinct to prevail, to tell her all would be well. When she finally slid into bed she felt herself tumble into sleep as if she were loose bricks spilling into an endless pit. By this time the husband had groggily awaked. "Whaswrong?" he mumbled. Within seconds he was snoring again.

The boy died precisely at noon two days later. His third-grade class was about to break for lunch when he suddenly lurched forward in his desk, cried aloud and collapsed onto the floor. The other children screamed. Their teacher realized the extent of the trouble and sought the principal's permission to dismiss them for the rest of the day. The police and an ambulance were called first, then the parents, who both worked. They arrived at the school in separate cars only to find that the ambulance had already left for a nearby hospital. The mother abandoned her car and allowed her husband to drive at breakneck speed to the emergency room. Usually she had to admonish him to slow down. He always drove too fast, which was why she often sat in the back seat with the boy.

The attending physician, a grizzled, sleepless man whose lower lip sagged, could only express his condolences. No cause of death was immediately discernible, and the physician seemed genuinely mystified. He dismissed epilepsy, given the teacher's report, and merely shrugged and shook his head. The teacher was on hand as well, weeping and hugging the mother. The father thought he was going to lose control and hurl himself at someone or throw chairs through windows or rush into the streets screaming. He could not stay still. He wanted to see his son. His son could not be dead. They'd been so happy, so lucky, so healthy. How could his son be dead? There was some mistake. No one was dead. Everyone was dead, but not his son. The mother and teacher wept. The physician sighed and stammered. Nurses offered coffee and soft drinks. They heard the word "autopsy." The boy was only eight years old.

The father tore off his necktie and threw it onto the floor, kicked at it with his shoe. Sweat had gathered at his temples. He was on fire. He was going to pass out. He pressed his back against a wall of lime green construction blocks and panted. He saw the physician's lower lip sag further and wanted to tear out his tongue.

The trip home seemed to pass in slow motion. The father stared ahead, wordless, while the mother gazed at trees and telephone poles floating by silently as clouds.

When they got home the first thing he saw on the foyer table was the green tube. It had not been touched since he'd set it there, mainly because everybody had been too busy to remember it. He seized the thing, noticing it had practically lost its glow, and rushed to the back yard to hurl it with all his strength into the wooded lot behind their house. He sank to the ground and howled. The mother had gone directly up to bed, although she knew she wouldn't sleep. She had to lie and think and sort things out, to fathom this new immensity. "So this is how it comes," she repeated to herself as she tried to find a comfortable position. Yet for all her need to understand, she found she could not concentrate. Her thoughts raced ahead of each other and collided in some murky abyss where nothing made any sense. She tried to form an image of her son's face but no image came.

Louis Gallo

During the months that followed the father and mother rarely discussed the boy. Nor had the doctors found any convincing cause of death despite some talk of a brain virus. The mother welcomed friends and sympathy but the father refused to see anyone, took leave from his job and indulged himself in long solitary walks through the neighborhood park. He refused to let his wife clear out the child's room as she had planned, it seemed to him, almost immediately. He insisted the room remain exactly as it was, and he padlocked it to make sure it would. The mother never asked for the key. He even heard her laugh on occasion with friends or on the telephone. He refused to allow her to attend to any insurance or routine police matters concerning the boy's death; these he took upon himself, ponderously, with an almost religious zeal. It was as if he had assumed the death his personal and private loss. In darker moments he spoke to the dead boy and promised that he would keep his room clean.

The mother started going out with friends, volunteering her spare time to work with patients at the Children's Hospital and, in general, getting on with life. She even found herself flirting with some men she worked with. She entertained the prospect of a brief affair. She rarely thought about her son and would not look at pictures in the family album, which the father looked at every night. It occurred to her that time had stopped for him, that he would always think of their son as only recently dead, that his own life had become a kind of shrine to the boy. It seemed that the father was untouchable in his grief. Only rarely would he speak; nor would he answer the telephone or letters piling up urgently on his desk.

Six months later, after the mother had her affair and found a better job, which was imperative since the father never returned to his, she came home early one afternoon to run some errands. The day before she had gone to a salon and paid handsomely for a complete facial; she had also trimmed her hair. She gazed at her new image in the mirror, pleased with herself, when she realized that the father was not puttering around the house as usual. It dawned on her that she was no longer a mother or wife. The shock sent her spiraling about the house in search of her husband. She wanted to shake him, scream at him, threaten him, give an ultimatum. She was in love with another man. The past did not exist.

She thought he might be out in the back yard where he had begun a small flower garden, but she could not find him. She called; there was no response. Then she thought she saw a white patch of his shirt in the back lot, an abandoned place overgrown with weeds and bushes. She crept silently toward the shirt and saw the father on his knees mumbling incoherently. She remembered the same look in her son. He did not seem to notice her, so she moved closer until she was practically upon him. He was arranging small stones in a circle around the plastic glow stick, which had been thrust into the ground vertically so that it rose up as a kind of obelisk. She could distinguish their son's name in his mumbling. Rather than make a scene, she stole silently away. What she had seen had made her queasy. She threw up several times before sliding into bed and burying herself under the covers.

Later that night, equipped with flashlight and shovel, she made her way cautiously toward the indecent memorial. She balanced the flashlight on a nearby rock and began to scatter the pebbles the father had so meticulously arranged. She too was now on her knees before the demonic tube. The face of her son suddenly appeared to her and tears swelled her eyes It was the first time since his death that she could picture him so clearly. She stroked the damp earth surrounding the tube and wiped it onto her face.

"Forgive me," she implored as the image of the boy began to recede. She seized the tube and inserted it down her blouse until it rested full length against her chest.

"Mine," she groaned, "mine."

She rocked slowly as she kneeled, humming an old song she'd learned from her grandmother. The full moon made her new face glow. A minstrelsy of insects screeched in the background. The shadows of dark, foreboding trees reminded her of ancient spirits returning for homage.

In her distraction she had failed to hear the father's footsteps approaching, and when she turned to meet his empty, violent, terrible eyes, it was already too late.

Italian

Grandma arranged four chipped, glazed bowls on the surface of her porcelain kitchen table, one pooled with olive oil, another piled with screaming red pimentos, in the third a mound of shriveled capers, in the fourth, potent anchovies unrolled and spread flat like veneer.

Grandfather cut a toasted slice of bread, dipped one side of each half in the oil until saturated, added two anchovies apiece with a sprinkling of capers and pimento. He pressed together the half sandwich and passed it to me or Ruthie or our parents or whoever begged the most.

He made one after another until everyone had enough, the flock fed. When it was his turn, he took his time. That bread floated in the oil almost, but not quite, for good. Then the capers and pimento burst out of his mouth as he bit into the coppery bodies of fish.

We watched his face proclaim the right taste, the joy and graceful ease of a minor perfection unglued from time. Only later would we know *exactly* how good those sandwiches tasted, when we tried but failed to recreate them ourselves.

We surmised a missing ingredient, some essence of our grandfather, corporealized, passed through his fingers into the concoctions. Some aura or soul spice. He was a sly one all right.

New Shirt

I n 1954 my Uncle Alphonse took the bus to Goldberg's Men's Clothiers on Poydras Street where he bought a new Arrow dress shirt, sparkling white with stern isosceles collars. It cost three dollars, a lot of money in those days. He unfolded it, picked out each pin meticulously and flapped it back and forth for airing. He hung it on a sturdy wooden hanger and told Aunt Cecile he would wear it only on special occasions.

He didn't wear the new shirt to his birthday party in 1954, four months after he bought it. He said the shirt was more important than any birthday, especially at his age. Nor did not wear it on Easter Sunday to church nor to his fortieth anniversary of marriage nor to Christmas mass or the New Year's Eve party. Uncle Alphonse did not wear his new shirt in 1954 but he dropped some moth balls into its front pocket and routinely admired its texture, brilliance and fresh starchy smell. In 1955 he did not wear the shirt to his first grandson's baptism—and again, not on his birthday, Easter or Christmas.

He didn't wear the shirt in 1956 or 57, 58, 59, to observe the death of Stalin or the Korean, War, Ike's re-election, Elvis on Ed Sullivan, the invention of tranquilizers, Civil Rights, the Interstate Highway program, the launching of Sputnik. "He's waiting for the new decade," Aunt Cecile chuckled. But on New Year's Day 1960 Uncle appeared in one of his fuzzy, old and slightly faded flannels. "This isn't the right time," he mumbled gloomily.

The shirt had become a family joke by now. Uncle Alphonse did not celebrate Kennedy's election, the Beatles in New York, Viet Nam, the assassinations, Chicago, Watts, the hippies, Neil Armstrong's giant leap, not in his new white shirt anyway.

In the seventies Uncle did not wear the shirt when the war ended, when Nixon resigned and Jimmy Carter lusted in his heart, when Disco killed rock and roll or during the Bicentennial.

He had become morose and secretive about the shirt, hid it in the darkest corner of the closet, sealed it in black plastic, sprayed it with mist to stave off dry rot. He did not wear his shirt to Ronald

Reagan's inauguration, nor to the baptisms and confirmations of more grandchildren, the funeral of his mother and Aunt Cecile's operation. When the Soviet Union collapsed, the shirt still looked new, flawless and elegant, though perhaps a bit quaint.

And here's where I come in—Uncle first let me see it around this time. He'd taken a fancy to me and sensed I would understand— I did, even if it's hard to explain. When the fishhook started to shred Uncle's gut and Chernobyl exploded, he turned yellow and coughed a lot, told me in a rare moment of levity that his skin would never match the shirt now. And something else: "Don't let them bury me in it. What's so special about death? Wear a new white shirt only when something really grand happens." They buried him in a black suit and blue turtleneck sweater. Aunt Cecile had already given me the shirt. "He wanted you to have it," she said. "I thought we might see him wear it to the Resurrection, but I guess I was wrong." Now it hangs in my closet, pristine as moonlight, immune to time, beautiful.

It won't surprise me to wait forever but one of these days something really grand is bound to happen. The moth balls are still pungent.

La Belle Dame Sans Merci

I met her at the designated hour of midnight at the antiquated corner bar, The Napoleon House, a place legend has it that supporters of the Emperor planned to deposit after they rescued him from St. Helena's. Well, now it's a hangout for artists, poets, musicians, hangers on, even politicians. The Ramos Gin Fizzes are pretty bad, but if you sit at a battered table in the back room you can control the old phonograph and play whatever classical record you crave. I sat up front because someone had commandeered the music and played a lot of Poulenc, Dvorak and Eric Satie.

I arrived early of course, not because I rejoiced at the idea of meeting a beautiful lesbian who planned to chew me out for abandoning her friend, but because I had nothing else to do. So I ordered a succession of vodka martinis and shot glasses of green chartreuse. I piddled with napkins, wrote a few lines in my journal, proceeded to get so drunk that nothing anyone could say would phase me, not even, we're all dying, friend, start praying. I knew I'd feel shitty the next day but, hell, the next day was upon us, behind the curtain, a twist of the doorknob, the lifting of a veil.

So she shows up, let's call her Sappho, I like that name, I like the original's poetry—I burn, yeah, I burn too— and she wears a slinky, tight fitting shift I think they call them, garnet necklace and ear rings, patent leather shoes, and, naturally, I brim with desire for the unattainable— she has made a mission of denunciating men— but she's here to dress me down for hurting her friend who, by the way, is heterosexual. She orders a glass of house Chablis because, she says, it's cheap and she doesn't want to get drunk, not tonight. "Can you go put on some Bach?" she asks. No, I can't. Some dork controls the music. So she gets right to the point, calls me despicable, that her friend—let's call her Rafaela— was really crazy about me and I just disappeared after spending an afternoon with her when we lay on the grass on the bank of one of the park lagoons, I reading Yeats to her, she listening, her hand stroking my hip. "Why didn't you make love to her?" Sappho demands to know. And on she went, castigating me mercilessly, I the mouse to her cat.

I thought about defending myself, explaining that Rafaela was so gorgeous and perfect, so supple and kind that I felt terrified, that I feared plunging into fathomless depths, that she surpassed me, a Jaguar to my Ford Pinto, that I could not bear losing her once I had succumbed… and, moreover, I could not read her, had no idea she craved me, I saw only the cover of that book, the pages seemed glued shut, you know, that old game, the first-mover risks all, something like god creating creation and wondering what went wrong—

But I said nothing, decided to appease Sappho, the referee declaring a KO so she could spit in my face and denounce me to the world as a low, chauvinist son-of-a-bitch once and for all—which perhaps I am. In truth I was so zonked nothing mattered—call me a hero, a coward, a narcissistic wretch, what's the difference? Of a sudden the image of Rafaela on that bank, her pouty lips, her dazzling eyes, her soothing flesh… I relived it all, Sappho yapping away like some crazed insect, I tossed Yeats into the lagoon, embraced Rafaela and kissed her lips, yes, and she hugged me and we thrived, a recollection of eternity in one ambered second of the past, that vision, option, that redemption. Which is why the past is superior to the present, which is why the past justifies the future, which is why time is the river you can always step into twice.

The Arcs of the Covenant

They rock slowly on the porch swing, her head resting on his shoulder. She likes the way he fiddles with her hair, the silent contentment she feels at the moment, with him, alone, rocking in the night. But still she waits, all the same, in her secret urgent way. For he will speak, shatter the tranquil silence.

"I'd like to try some new food," he finally sighs, "fruit maybe, a cross between strawberries and mangos, something cool and tropical, no, unearthly, like a fruit from another planet, something luscious exploding in your mouth that tastes like outer space. A Jacuzzi full of herbs and perfumes from ancient Persia. Music too, cosmic, like Charles Ives's *The Unanswered Question* but better. What else? A beautiful woman, of course, and wine from the age of Mozart, so dry and fine it would taste like soft fire. Or something like that, something new, never before experienced by anybody. A massage too. We'd lounge in a redwood tub and the air would be laced with ice but not too cold. The stars would sparkle, and we'd stare at comets streaking across the blue-black sky. That's what I'd like right now."

The stiff swing bruises all of her soft spots, but she doesn't mind. He has wrapped his arm around her but seems as remote as the dissonant chords in that Ives music he always brings up at such moments. She is of many minds about his desires. She too wants to drift away, indulge her fantasies, but feels she cannot afford to, given his musings. Somebody has to stick around, play the anchor. It worries her when he starts thinking about weird fruits from other solar systems and wine that tastes like soft fire and, well, all of it. It means he will soon say that he is leaving for Belize or the rain forest or wherever else he believes he cannot be found.

She only half understands that Belize for him is only a word, a dream state, a flimsy hope for not only relief but release. She is too literal, he always says, whereas he revels in the frenzy of rhetoric, finds distraction from what bothers him most through mere articulation of the fabulous. Which is not to say that he might not on impulse dash off for the real place if things got too unbearable. But if he ever does leave, it will already be too late.

The beautiful woman business bothers her too. "It better be me," she laughs, "I'll kill you, old man. You get in a Jacuzzi with anybody but me and you're one dead geyser." She knows it bothers him when she brings up his age—twenty years her senior, but still only forty-two.

His fingers squeeze her shoulder tighter, but he seems no closer. It is his way of letting her know that she means the world to him, that if, say, he left without her, it would signify the death of him, that he'd be doing her a favor. He also knows she doesn't want to hear it, that she'd come to hate Belize, that his mere mention of it strikes a chord of anxiety that sets set her off in a torrent of defense.

As they rock the first fireflies of the season flicker in shrubbery along their walkway, ion-charged gusts batter the unicorn wind chimes, and squeaking bats swoop down from a darkened elm tree across the street. This is nice, she thinks, curling closer to him, why can't he see this is so nice? There isn't anything else, in fact; all the Jacuzzis and galactic fruit in the world wouldn't be any better than what they already have, if he'd only see it. So why can't he? Why is he so abstract, so strange? They can't just sit still and inhale the delicious world as it is, even if she herself can imagine improvements.

He attributes her way of thinking to the weary old sloped mountains of West Virginia, where, he says often enough, people just sit. They don't do anything… just sit. And there is no way he would ever understand how she can not only just sit but sit in darkness for hours. It would drive me out of my mind, he jokes often enough. She knows her sitting irritates him. Sometimes, when very tired, he joins her and relaxes and she can feel the tension flow out of his body. Those are the times she savors.

But when he is in a state, as she puts it, she can sense his disdain not for her, but for the sitting, for every knothole of the house. It does indeed distress him, but in truth she often taunts him with it deliberately, remains riveted in the dark as he rages and fumes and carries all of the furniture up and down the stairs. She tortures him with it because he hates it, because of Belize and beautiful women. But she also knows he'll be back, that his mania for order and justice and perfection will wear him down like a sad old draught horse, and he'll slink in to lie beside her, press her body into the sofa, his atop hers, deeply together, waiting for her gentle touch, a mere patch of flesh against flesh, her warmth, her serene acceptance of the walls of Jericho collapsing.

If she too seethes on the inside, it's too deep for him to grasp; he fears such depths, since his own distress is all surface, eruptive. He likes to think he can explode and then be done with it. She knows better. Or thinks she does.

She understands that his sadness is also deep, that the minor eruptions serve only to get him going, even if the going amounts to flinging a stone into the air. His eruptions are false, evasive, however much lava flows; he fights what he hates most and what has become his metaphor for hopelessness: sitting. In the dark. Not even waiting. Turning off but keenly attuned to the wing beats of the flimsiest moth.

What's the point? he'll ask. Why? We could paint the bathroom, fix the porch, change the tires, dig up the sewer pipes. We could do something. And he remembers what she can't—what he was before she knew him, when all the trouble came along. That, yes, he could in those days erupt and be done with it, ease himself into new tranquilities, pass the days not only in contentment but actual delight in even the most ephemeral pleasures. But only he knows this. How could she, so young, so unscathed? And then again if he has changed, what difference does it make? Some things change people so profoundly they no longer recognize themselves.

She will argue that you can't let the past destroy you. Why not? he always asks. Because I love you, she says. Which puts an end to philosophy. He loves her too, he might say, but suppose he is indeed ruined and therefore not good for her or anybody else? Suppose love is something delicate, like a mote suspended in a light beam, he might ask. Anything can come along to alter it. Just draw the shade, he could say, and the golden beam and mote disappear. But it's not what he wants to say; he cannot not put his finger on what he wants to say or how to say it, he who thinks of words as akin to physical sensations.

And so they rock in the night, in graceful arcs, on the swing, in this manner, her manner, as he confronts real and illusory hurdles blocking every direction he can imagine. And it is good, even if he can never sit as still as she sits, never stop clinging to her, never forget everything else.

First Love

This goes back to the Pleistocene and I'm all of thirteen in the first year of junior high, a hive full of thugs and hoodlums and insane maniacs where I definitely don't belong but my parents don't know any better and say I need experience so you can imagine the everyday terror like when I see one kid pull a .38-revolver from his pocket and brandish it around screaming, it's loaded…

…But there's bliss too, in band class when I see Stacey who is so far out of my league it's like glimpsing the edge of the universe though in fact she sits right next to me, second chair flute to my first, and she's a fully developed woman at thirteen and everyone agrees queen of the school and head majorette and twirler and dancer and whatever her reasons and against all odds she likes me and I of course adore her and when the band director Mr. Gendarvis taps the podium with his wooden stick to start a Sousa march she presses her thigh firmly against mine and I can hardly stand it and hope Mr. Gendarvis doesn't notice what's happening though how could he not?

The whole class period, our thighs fused together, imagine, even with that heavy Cor Jesu senior ring glued to her finger with wax, her boyfriend, Tommy, from the Catholic school, rumored the toughest hoodlum in all Gentilly, you don't mess with Tommy for any reason, much less his girlfriend, and yet…

…So this goes on for a few years and I'm finally sixteen with a learner's permit and I borrow my grandfather's golden Imperial with its legendary wings and spend five hours washing it for him and in return I can take Stacey out on a date in it so I rub every smudge from every window with Windex and scrub the white walls with Brillo pads until my fingers bleed, that's how obsessed I am and, by the way,

Stacey has broken up with Tommy and has chosen (that's exactly the word, chosen) a new boyfriend, Joey, and Tommy beats the hell out of him right in the school yard with everybody gathered round to watch like some Roman spectacle and Joey returns a few days later with black eyes, a broken jaw and his face swollen like a pumpkin but he doesn't care because now he's got Stacey and he's a hero by default and they walk through the corridors like royalty and I wonder if he will beat the hell out of me because I'm taking her out in my grandfather's Imperial which is really happening, despite Joey, and either he knows or doesn't care because I don't care, all I care about is Stacey, my first real love, my goddess...

...And I drive her out to the Point, this meager peninsular at West End that pokes out into Lake Pontchartrain and we pass the ancient light house, where the Point stops, and there's space for about fifty cars where everybody makes out and I've wanted to do this for three torturous years so I slide over on the seat and wrap my arm around her shoulders and she flicks away her Salem and I press my lips onto hers and I love it but know the kiss is no good, not really a kiss, because she keeps her lips to herself, clenched, and just sort of puts up with me messing around with them with my mouth and, oh God, three torturous years, those thighs fused to mine in band, her sweet smile, her everything.

But she's just putting up with it because she definitely does like me, I swear to that, but maybe not the way she liked Tommy or likes Joey which sort of bewilders me off because I just don't get it and I pull away and slide down low and rest my head on the seat and sigh really loud though I'm ignited inside and don't know what to do or say and she says nothing but lights up another Salem and asks if I want one but I say no, I don't smoke, and I didn't then, and suddenly I feel nauseous— her lips taste like ashes, and yet I will kiss ashes, lick ashes, eat ashes, smear my face with ashes, vomit ashes for more of her.

Pennies and Dandelions

I lie on the river embankment and let the sun drench my face. Chloe, who is seven, pokes about in the soccer field for dandelions to blow into my hair. She wants me to tickle her, so I shout, "Little girl, if you blow one more flower on me, I'm *really* going to tickle you." She giggles and squeals and searches all the more intently.

I don't merely enjoy the sun, I need it.

It's a lean season for dandelions, so she soon loses interest and mopes back toward me.

"Let's go smash some pennies—and a quarter," she says.

The train track is about fifty yards from the embankment, behind which flows the dark green New River. It is quiet today but I have seen it flood this very field, destroying everything. Today its surface merely glitters like gems.

I tell my daughter I want to lie here, so she can put pennies on the track. She likes the idea and digs into my pockets. We know the train will arrive in about thirty minutes. Otherwise I would not let her near the tracks. The day seems still, timeless, without the roar of engines.

I watch her place and replace the pennies meticulously on the rails. She cannot decide where to put the quarter for the best smash. We have flattened many coins during our last few days together. I have put them in an envelope so she can take some "home" to her friends halfway across the continent. On the best ones you can still see Lincoln's face, distorted and ghostly.

I know I will come here again when she's gone. I will see her skipping in the field, sprinting up the embankment to the river, throwing rocks into the water. I'll see her take off her sandals and wade into the river to collect pebbles. I will hear her calling me. She will pick the greatest dandelion ever and rush for me, still lying in the sun, and blow it into my hair. I hope it rains down like nuggets of warm snow that bury me entirely. Then, when she least expects it, I'll break free, explode from my tomb of dandelion fur, and tickle her. She won't be here, but the brutal engines will always rumble onward, crush endless rows of pennies. For my eyes.

Bedtime Story to My Daughter on the Eve of Divorce

Your hair blazes even in moonlight. I am late—forgive me, I had obligations. The lawyers, you know. It is unpardonable that I should miss our story time. You are sleeping fitfully, a nightmare, and have flung back the covers. It is far too warm for a flannel nightgown, but I won't wake you, would like nothing better than to wake you up and treat you to a surprise pizza and Coke, but our schedules are now proscribed. We cannot deviate because it might make trouble tomorrow. We must never suspect it might make tomorrow memorable, even joyous—the time Daddy and I got up in the middle of the night and danced or sang a duet or watched cartoons on TV. I myself have such memories. Little snippets of time. Our pasts are kaleidoscopes, nothing ever completely connecting. But there are privileged moments, like the time I cut off a strand of my grandmother's silver hair with her own scissors. "You'll make me bald like your grandpa!" she cried in secret delight, feigning outrage, but crawling after me on all fours as I breathlessly escaped. We had broken the rules, which is what we'd remember... the breaking, not the rules.

So I'll tell you a story now, when you can't hear it, when you're asleep. You will never hear another like it. It may disturb you as it disturbs me, may even terrify you but you won't hear it, so I'll spare you the truth even in the telling. Because this is a story about monsters, not the flimsy, make-believe ghouls and beasts of cartoons and fairy tales, but real monsters in black suits with legal writs, the only monsters. And its moral is *goodbye*, little one.

Once upon a time...

Honeysuckle and Sweet Olive

Grandma told us that it officially began when he said he wanted a little boy sailor suit for his birthday. He said he always got new cloths on his birthday and holidays, like the crinkly seersucker on Easter when he made his communion or the striped flannel pajamas for Christmas. She had noticed signs all along but kept them to herself: he dropped things, forgot what day it was, couldn't find his way to the bank or Southern Radio, where he practically lived. "Not all the time," she said, blowing out some extra air so that her lips buzzed like a small motor, "just every now and then. But enough to worry me. I didn't say anything because it would make him mad. He said he had too much to remember and the days were shorter. 'They're stealing a little more time each day,' he said, shaking his head. 'Who's they?' I asked. He just sighed and told me I knew what he was talking about."

I remember the day of her announcement. We had finished up the Sunday lunch and were loitering at the table, picking at a little more crumb cake, a little more pecan pie, just sort of making pigs of ourselves. Grandpa left the room suddenly—he looked sort of dazed—and went for his nap. He didn't tell the usual World War I stories or even excuse himself; he stood up, gazed at us as if he had never seen us before, and started out. He looked skinny and fragile and his fingers trembled a little. We all knew something was wrong, except maybe my sister Ruthie, who was still too young. Mom and dad looked at each other with raised eyebrows. I had seen a few old people get skinny all of a sudden, like Uncle Ambrose, and they didn't last long after that. Grandma came in from the kitchen, where she had taken some dishes, wiped her hands, and sat down in her husband's chair. She had never done that before. Grandpa's chair at the head of the table was sacred.

"I have something to say," she began, "and you're not going to like it."

"I think we know already, Ma," Dad said. He looked sad as an old rag. Dad was devoted to his father.

She ignored him. "Grandpa is sick. His mind's going. It's like he's daft. Yesterday he went out the door in his underwear. He said he was driving up see Alphonse at Southern. When I told him he needed to put on some clothes, he blew up, told me to mind my own business. But he walked back into the bedroom and put on some clothes anyway. He stormed out of the house and slammed the door like I was his worst enemy. Not ten minutes later he came back.

"'Can't find my keys' is all he said and then sank into this very chair and stared at the wall. I don't think he knew where he was. 'Maybe we ought to see a doctor,' I said. Well, he understood that all right and exploded again.' I'm all right!' he shouted and pounded the table. Then he belched—you know those big cochons he makes and smiled and everything seemed normal again. Except his shirt was buttoned up wrong and he wore two different shoes on his feet. 'Jake,' I said, 'I know you're all right, but it wouldn't hurt to see Dr. Mosby. You need to see him about your heart anyway.' Well, he started to rant and rave about how I wanted to get rid of him and how I fed him the wrong food and it wasn't him but the blood pressure medicine. Then he put his head down on the table and went to sleep. Just like that. So what I'm telling you all is that Grandpa is ill, and he needs to see Dr. Mosby, and I can't do it all myself. I'm so stiff with the rheumatism as it is."

And then, for the first time in my life, I saw my grandmother cry. She twiddle with a linen napkin and wept softly. "He's getting so old right before my eyes."

"What's the matter, Grandma?" Ruthie asked.

Grandma reached over with her gnarled fingers and pat Ruthie's hand. "It's ok, sweetheart," she said, "your grandpa just needs to go to the doctor."

"Is Grandpa ok?" Ruthie asked. She had not digested a bit of what her grandmother had just said.

"I'll make the appointment," Dad said. "He's not going to like it."

"He'll fight you and make you feel like scum," Grandma said.

"Can I come too?" I asked.

Dad smiled. He looked older too and seemed beaten down. "No, Jakie," he said, "it's not a fun place to go."

"But I don't want Grandpa to be sick."

"None of us do, Jakie," Grandma said. "He's an old man though Old people are always sick."

"Are you sick, Grandma?" Ruthie asked, as if suddenly she knew the family had changed.

"Oh, I just have my usual rheumatism and hay fever. My feet hurt so much."

And that's the first time we heard that too. Grandma came from a long line of stalwart forebears who refused to complain about anything. Their hands might be burned to char and they would remain dignified and poised and go on chatting as if valentines throbbed above their heads. So if Grandma admitted that her feet hurt, they must have hurt so bad that none of the rest of us would have been able to stand it for one minute, much less year after year.

I remember looking at the screen door. One edge of the mesh had come loose and had curled up at the joint. The metal latch hung down like a tiny anchor. Sunlight eased through lace curtains that had begun to dry rot. I felt massive forces at work, forces over which none of us had any control, and I stormed out of the room, out the door and plopped down on the concrete steps of the small porch. I tried to think about everything Grandma had said, but I couldn't. My mind had gone blank, maybe like my grandfather's. I heard the bells gong over at St. Rosa de Lima. The scents of honeysuckle and sweet olive wafted in the breezes. The tall wooden fence that separated Grandma's house and the one next door looked soggy, gray and soft. Just a few years before I had climbed that fence with abandon. I realized then that I would never climb it again, nor did I want to climb it. Something new had begun, something I didn't like and wanted to push away like a big rock suddenly appearing in the yard. Whatever was going on seemed inexorable. And we had to live with it though it would hurt and diminish us all.

Recruitment with Bosco

We're off visiting one college after another so my daughter can decide for the Fall. A zealous student tour guide leads us along varied walkways of a rather dumpy campus (though parts are Jeffersonian impressive). The guide walks backwards to face us, a rather morose group of twelve or so parents and students. She banters chipperly about the diversity of the school.

Suddenly, as if out of nowhere, this pooch, a sort of battered Boston terrier, trots briskly towards our group, a mutt aging along with the rest of us, rather filthy and mottled. He's in the distance but gaining on us, and it's his serious intent amuses me, all business, as if he's part of the group now, which he is. He trots along right beside me, tongue flapping as he huffs, short stubby tail awag, and he and I make eye contact. That's it, we're partners now; he keeps looking at me, and I return the gaze and start to laugh, in fact, I can't stop laughing although I try to stifle it as a cough but it's obvious I'm laughing and the guide gives me an evil eye since I imagine she thinks I'm laughing at her. But no, the dog (whom I've named Bosco after that awful concoction my mother made me drink as a child)…

…But it's not even Bosco I'm laughing at making mock of our entire enterprise here by imitating us! It's us, we, a group on somber business involving lots of money, and here's Bosco, jaunting along, for five buildings. Sticking close to me, he refuses to actually enter any of the buildings; he merely waits for us to finish and exit. The guide has tried to give him the slip by exiting on the rear side of where we are now, the gymnasium, and I am dismayed that the ruse has worked—

But wait! Here comes Bosco spinning round the corner of the edifice, racing toward us, the guide who has ignored Bosco all this time now shooting venomous glances his way. I lag behind the group so Bosco can catch up, which he does, impervious, cocky, all canine smiles as he glances adoringly at me. But sad to say, we're back at the bursar's office and must leave Bosco behind, which he senses. He takes one sniff, turns away, gives me a last backward glance and ambles away…. I see another tour group across campus and he heads their way.

Louis Gallo

    I like to think I made a friend this day, a goofy little creature who, merely by existing, puts all of our grand enterprises to shame.

    On the drive home at sunset I start to laugh again and my wife and girls laugh and no doubt Bosco, still on campus, never stops laughing as he sinks his teeth into the marrow of that juicy bone we call wisdom.

Ablative Absolute, or, Quest for Mind

O f the countless things I have now forgotten, arguably the most irrelevant, inconsequential and downright *small* is that musty grammatical construct, the ablative absolute. I recall a year of mild suffering during which I studied it—first and second semesters, sophomore rank, Tulane University—the class (Latin 101), the teacher (an authentic Italian with the lugubrious name of Mr. Casanova, ABD, who was short and burdened with heavy bluish Nixon-like beard when freshly shaved—he used Canoe, my brand back then—the room (Newcomb Hall 406), the faces and names of my fellow students on all four sides, which I won't bother to record here, although I understand two are already dead, one blown up in Viet Nam long ago, the other a victim of some gruesome disease that petrifies the entrails... I even remember the color of the walls (Dannon coffee yogurt), the hour (one p.m., right after lunch), my next class (Greek Mythology with Dr. Regenos, surely the most cantankerous, pedantic and *old* human being alive at the time, a smoldering Tithonus), the girl I strained to sit next to (Joyce Bergen from Troy, New York, who, despite her miraculous, creamy body, I was convinced had a wooden leg). I remember everything except the wretched ablative absolute. It is as if, alone among a myriad of closely related mnemonic tidbits, it chose self-extinction for the sole purpose of vexing me decades later. It cannot be argued that I have forgotten, in this case, what is not worth remembering; if so, I should have forgotten the coffee yogurt-colored walls as well. Nor have I forgotten because of the suffering I endured, which, as I recall, would confirm the psychoanalytic voo doo of hysterical repression. I agonized far more in Introduction to Physics, yet I recall with pristine clarity the formula for the caloric disintegration (i.e., melting) of an accelerating snowball of x mass which collides with a brick wall at y degrees Celsius. So neither irrelevance nor hysteria can account for my inability to remember the purpose, structure and significance of the ablative absolute. Hence I take my forgetting as portentous, a worrisome sign indeed, a good old-fashioned fray in the rope.

Louis Gallo

I have forgotten much else, true—human demographics during the Age of Constantine, the specifics of the Mexican-American War, most of the periodic table, the horror of logarithms, and so on—but it is always the ablative absolute that returns to haunt me at the oddest moments, say, when comparing prices of toilet tissue in Kroger or spreading Plastic Wood into cracks in my worn, woeful weatherboards. Most recently the forgetting seized me as I drove home after an abortive foray to the video store. Back then I had spent hours, days, weeks studying the ablative absolute because I knew it would be something I would forget, because it defied reason and therefore required arduous concentration, because I had no interest in it whatever except to pass my language requirement courses. You could say I pounded the ablative absolute into my soul with a sledge hammer, yet still… This bodes no good for memory, does it, or intellect or reason or that sine qua non of human evolution, the neo-cortex? If we forget what we pound into our souls, can we expect any less, or more, from that which we acquire casually, say, from CNN factoids or *Time* magazine Milestones? Might we not also forget our greatest moments of triumph, our darkest nights of grief and loss?

…Indeed, if we forget the ablative absolute, I maintain that we can forget our own mothers, our names, our very personalities and birthrights. In the end mere amorphous existence would prevail, dimly conscious of itself, mollusk-like and gaseous at once. We would be no better off than mist, which, of course, assumes that we are in fact better off than mist, a position I endorse but refuse to pursue. Thus have I undertaken to retrieve the ablative absolute from the intricate curlicues of memory-fold in which it has undoubtedly enshrouded itself. Everything else goes on hold until I remember. I have spent four days and three nights literally locked in my study, straying out only to eat and go to the bathroom. I am not one of those ascetic mystics who can function when deprived of food and water; I have no interest in visions or hallucinations, the cotton-candy of tender minds; I reject all consolation. It is the ablative absolute or nothing. As for the ablative relative, should such a monstrosity exist, feed it to the buzzards. I curse compromise, always a ruse for the sake of practicality, as Abel cursed Cain, if he cursed Cain; and if he didn't, he should have. Absolutely.

I have accumulated enough sick days to make even a two- or three-week stint at remembrance possible. I have left a message on my answering machine suggesting (only suggesting, to thwart thieves) that

I am in the bathroom. I've informed my fiancé, Isidore, that I need a vacation, some, as they say, "personal space," to clear my head. So all is well, and I can concentrate. The problem is I'm getting nowhere—nearly four full days of acute, intense recall, and not a shred on insight into the ablative absolute Other interesting residues have returned—my earliest memory is not, as I'd previously thought, excreting upon myself while in a stroller on North Miro Street in New Orleans pushed my god-mother Aunt Sylvia, but rather watching my little sister excrete upon herself in *her* stroller. The sight itself is not even the memory; my overwhelming *feeling* of revulsion is the memory. I am beginning to think that individual, discreet memories, rank secondary to the primary gut- work of overall sensation. That is, perhaps a Polaroid-like scene, whether prolonged or merely a flash in the night, merely cue us in to something more fundamental, like feelings, appetites, fears, desires, pain, pleasure. If this is the case, my quest for the ablative absolute, and any other pure byte of information, will abort before it begins. Could it be that I, one of the few remaining Platonists in the universe, have discovered the truth of nostalgia and reminiscence in a single false maneuver by remembering not my sister but my own gagging over her sweet, acrid, blossoming, fetid caca? And if so, the caca may as well have been mine as hers, may as well been anybody's. Absolute caca.

So we're in this bind, you see: the thing itself, quiddity, or the recoiling from the thing? I may well have to terminate my quest if this sort of mental mayhem persists. Meanwhile, I won't budge, except for necessities as I've mentioned—I'm no martyr—until the ablative absolute re-reveals and reconstitutes itself to me exactly as I memorized it nearly three decades ago. Because I know it's there, taunting, teasing, aching to be grasped, like a naughty cheerleader in the distance. And if it's not there, fuck nostalgia and all the rest of it, for it would mean that nothing matters, that we should seize the moment as the insufferable hedonists whom I detest preach, that time and memory are gigantic hoaxes perpetrated by hopelessness. At least that's what I think it would mean. That's what it would mean for me. The destruction of one single atom of experience or sensation, like a black hole in our being, would suck our very plenum into itself eventually. And then where would we be but mired in fatal gravity? Hence, I labor for all mankind, for the universe itself. My work is precarious. I have roughly thirteen days, before sick leave runs out, to reach El Dorado. After that, one way or another, we can go our merriest of way, catch frisbees without teeth.

Dog Day

So I'm crossing campus one fine Wednesday, pure confection, no slack anywhere. I hum a ditty that has clung to me like wet sugar all week as I spot in the distance this red-haired mutt cantering heatedly as if he's the first of his species to have attained reason. Students swim out of classrooms like fish. I'm surrounded by youthful blue-jeaned hominids.

The dog is still distant but moving fast. his trajectory tells me I'm the one, despite this array of prime flesh. No, I muse, can't be me, don't know the beast. The kid next to me maybe or this long-legged vision I'm behind and want to stay behind. Anyway, he gains momentum each moment, and soon I know I am indeed the target.

He's a cylinder of ferocious zeal. An almost holy pain throbs in my ankle as books fly high and papers blow scatter and blow away. He seems permanently attached, even as I kick to paralyze. I finally connect with his jaw and knock some teeth out onto the lawn. He seems stunned, deranged with disappointment. We sit beside each other panting. He looks into my eyes with adoration.

"Why me, fella?" I wail. "Did I ever wrong you? Now I need shots."

I pat my wound, get up and limp away, the dog trotting behind, forever mine now that we have removed little pieces from each other.

This Little Piggie

Professor Paul Derbees felt he should object, in principle at least, even if he really did not mind the idea of sleeping beside his son at the campus day-care center. In fact, he took it as an opportunity to get closer to the boy. The attendants had complained that David refused to settle down at nap time, and, worse, his relentless whimpering had begun to disturb the other children. All parties finally agreed that one parent should occupy a cot beside David and hold his hand until he either slept or stopped crying. Magda could not possibly leave her office since she worked full time as a court reporter, but Paul had ample spare time between university classes.

"Sure it's unusual," admitted, Millie Thompson, the ebullient center director, "but we're creative here. We take nothing for granted."

The professor felt somewhat awkward on the first day as he lay beside an immensely comforted David. His cot seemed so massive and alien compared to the children's. Nor did it comfort him to know that grown women, including one of his own students, sat in the glass-plated teacher lounge observing the group. "If this gets around," Paul thought. But the love gushing from his two-year-old son's eyes as they lay facing each other compensated for any anxiety and embarrassment. He held the boy's fingers gently and sang to him, in a whisper of course, some sad ballads by Peter, Paul and Mary.

It amazed him to recall later that both he and Paul had drifted off almost instantly. Nap time fell between one and two, and he attributed his own sleepiness to digestion. He usually took a nap around five, after classes, which kept him up all night, and was pleased that the earlier nap made retiring at midnight not only possible but pleasurable. And David seemed absolutely radiant now that he slept well. Paul sympathized with his son's former insomnia since for years it had victimized him too—but all that was over now. Magda, who always went to bed around midnight, also liked the change. "We're a family again," she sighed happily, "and all because you're in day care, Paul."

One afternoon, when the university had cancelled classes (Paul had always streaked off after naps to meet his two o'clock course), Paul stuck around for band. "It revs them up again," said Millie. About twenty kids sat around banging on every manner of toy drum, triangle, wooden block, even garbage pail lids. They loved it. Paul figured, well, what the hell, why not? He snatched a stick from the floor and began beating his attaché case. Wary at first, the children soon accepted him as one of their own. Millie humored him afterward with "That was fun, wasn't it?" He sensed a subtle tone of disapproval curdle in her voice.

Paul began to arrive earlier so he could share the lunch experience with his son and the other children. He sat on one of the miniature chairs with them and made funny animal sounds, as they did. Sometimes he and the kids swapped cookies or juice. He recited funny poems and stories, made goofy faces. For some reason, though, he began to have difficulty sleeping on cue, which bothered David, who slept now only when certain his father was asleep nearby. Many of the children writhed without their binkies, so Paul humbled himself and requested one from Millie. She merely blinked her eyes and passed a spare pacifier into his fingers. He curled up on the cot, arranged the blanket and stuck the binkie into his mouth. Within minutes both he and David were out cold sucking on their binkies.

"I don't know if I like this binkie business," Magda complained one night when she caught him slipping it into his mouth in their bed.

"It works" is all he mumbled and rolled over to sleep.

Pretty soon Paul and his son arrived at nine every morning so they could participate in cutting and pasting, story time, outside play and numbers and words. "I didn't realize how little I understood about numbers and words," he confessed to Magda, alarmed about Millie's report that her husband had resorted to toddler babble during his hours in day care.

"He pronounces 'yellow' 'leddo,'" Millie had said. "But I'm afraid to kick him out. The kids love him."

After naps Paul started to roll out of his cot and crawl to band. All of the children could walk, but some still crawled when they chose, and the professor found it safe and easy. He crawled to Millie's desk one day and said, "Whazzaaat?" pointing to her necklace.

Millie stared and said, "Necklace," pronouncing the word with more than usual volume and articulation. She cleared her throat and asked Paul if he were taking his role a little too seriously. Paul squinted and huffed through his nose. He reached up and tried to snatch the necklace.

"Really, Paul, stop!" Millie cried.

The professor's eyes widened, he stared at the woman and started to howl.

"We had to literally hold him in our laps, Magda," she reported later to Paul's wife, "and pat his back and tell him it was ok. I even had to let him fondle my wretched necklace."

When Magda confronted Paul later that night, he sank to the floor and began to kick his feet. "Da-da, Da-da," he wailed. Magda found herself saying, much to her horror, "It's ok, Paulie, your Da-da isn't home right now. He'll be back later. Calm down, little guy."

She inserted a binkie into his mouth as he lay distraught on the floor, heaving his chest, his arms and legs spread wide. Tears puddled in his eyes. His speech was garbled because of the pacifier, but Magda could make out the words "kit cat," "leddo," and "di-pee."

"Paul, you *didn't!*" she exclaimed.

"Di-pee," cried the professor, wailing once again. The only consolation, later, was Magda's playing "This little piggie" with his toes. Paul squealed with delight when she got to the pinkie.

It was a turning point, of course, and from that day on Paul's satchel always contained a few gigantic diapers, along with the Juicy Juice and Oreos and peanut-and-jelly sandwiches. He would also not leave the house without ZZ, a cuddly stuffed zebra he had pilfered from David's pile of toys. Sometimes he and David fought over ZZ, but David always relented; he thought having his dad in day-care with him was wonderful.

Paul had abandoned his classes, to the dismay of an administration which the previous year had bestowed upon him a prestigious Excellence in Teaching award. Magda and Millie were called in for a conference and told that tenure did not protect any professor from outright negligence. "And from what I hear," coughed a senior vice president, "Paul needs serious help."

In this manner substantial plans were made for Paul's future. But it seemed appropriate that he finish out the semester at daycare in order to avoid disrupting the children. As for Paul, he cared only about getting to the red snare drum before Becky Wilson. She was quick for a girl—and mean. And he loved the days when Magda packed gummy bears into his lunch pail.

Magda felt some relief when Millie informed her that Paul had made excellent progress with his alphabet. "He has trouble with M's and W's," she sighed, "but who doesn't? And the lower case totally defeats him. Give it time."

"My lawyer thinks I should divorce and then adopt him," Magda sighed. "Is he faking it, you think?"

"I've never seen a happier man… child, that is. Faking it? Then he deserves an Academy Award."

"Well," Magda shrugged, "it could be worse—he could have gotten *old*."

Millie recoiled, raised her eyebrows in distaste. "But it's perverse," she cried. "He's unnatural and disgusting. A grown man. You'd think—"

Magda closed her eyes and dreamed of the second child she and Paul had always wanted but could never have. "Anybody messes with my kids…" she declared, "I'll hunt them down to the ends of the earth. You know how we mothers are. Lose a husband, gain a child. Who's complaining?"

La Petite Mort

Old professor Reno, many years retired, hobbled down Magazine Street with his meager bag of groceries. He wondered if he would make it home in the scorching New Orleans heat of August. If so, well then, life was good. Good had come to mean merely persisting another day, given his failing, precarious heart.

Professor Reno had returned to the city of his birth some twelve years earlier with a station wagon full of the only possessions he still prized—as well as a modest pension, which he had opted for in lump sum. Two divorces and interminable child support payments had just about cleaned him out. With the little money he had left he purchased a modest cottage on one of the side streets off Magazine. Not a good neighborhood but not entirely frightful either.

Every window on the block had bars and iron grill-work security gates bolted across both front and back doors. The place had cost Reno every cent, so he survived entirely on social security now. He had outlived most of his relatives, and his children had scattered across the country and rarely communicated with him. The old man felt that he barely existed, that he amounted to what the locals here called lagniappe, a little extra. And he knew, of course, that each of his days had its number.

He waited for the light at Jefferson, crossed the street cautiously and turned left at the next corner. Only half a block more to the small, dilapidated bungalow that hadn't been painted in thirty years. He fingered the keys in his pockets, took deliberate deep breaths, wiped sweat from his forehead with his fingers. I will make it, he urged himself. He planned to plunge into the easy chair in front of the television, rest, then heat up a can of Progresso chicken and barley soup. It must have been a little after one o'clock. The empty streets, stifling, painful with glare. He signed with relief as he trudged the steps onto his front porch, which, infested with termites, still supported his frail hundred and forty pounds.

He aimed the point of his key toward the lock as usual only to find that the door was already open. His first thought—I've been robbed.

Only a matter of time in this area. He entered the living room, saw no signs of vandalism and wondered if he had again merely forgotten to lock the door.

He sank into the easy chair in a state of joyous exhaustion. He had clung to another day; he had procured food; his legs had supported him all the way to the grocery and back. He might have nodded off easily except for an unusual sound–almost a heavy breathing–coming from the dark hallway that ran the length of the house. Were the robbers still inside? Not that it mattered. The little strength he retained made it impossible for him to investigate, or care. No, he would go to sleep for a while, nap, then heat up the soup.

But the sound intensified. He swiveled the chair toward the hallway and felt no surprise whatever to see a human figure emerge from its shadows. He wondered why he felt no fear and merely grunted, "Who is it?"

The figure stepped into the light so Professor Reno could get a good look at him. An old man, perhaps his age or a little younger. Gaunt yet tall and weighty, the intruder stepped closer. He carried some sort of machine and clear plastic tubes ran into his nose. Oxygen, the professor understood: the man was dying. It occurred to him that the visitor was an angel of death, or of mercy, it didn't matter.

"Who are you?" he asked meekly.

The visitor seemed agitated and angry. "My name is William Rennick," he growled. "I don't supposed that means a thing to you."

"I'm sorry," Professor Reno shook his head. "Perhaps a few clues? Do I know you?"

"Celeste Rennick," the tall man said. "That should ring a bell."

The professor searched his mind as if it were a long empty highway. "I've forgotten quite a bit," he attempted to chuckle, "at my age, you know. I don't know any Celeste."

And then the highway abruptly ended and he saw her, beckoning him as she had then, so long ago, in the Midwest, where he had pursued his graduate studies. She looked radiant, still the same young woman who wore fuzzy, tight sweaters, even in summers. She had not aged a year, a minute. er smile, bounteous, serene, sensuous. But ah, only a memory, a spot of time returned to work its magic.

"Dear sir," Professor Reno said, "yes, yes, yes… how could I forget Celeste? I knew her, yes, so long ago, so long ago. And do you come with news about my old friend? I do hope she remains well."

"William Rennick," the man sneered. "My name is William Rennick. Celeste's husband, husband now and husband then, when you knew her. She passed away last year, my wife, and I vowed to track you down should that occur. I'm not an articulate man as you were with your literary flourishes, attracting thousands of students. I studied engineering. But you… ah, the conquests, the fans, the women. They thought you were god."

"I was only a graduate student teaching a few classes when I knew Celeste. We had a few classes together." The professor began to feel positively chilled. He looked at the tall man's grizzled, dour and decimated face.

"You made love to my wife, professor, over and over, night after night. She told me she had to go over to the library to do research. You met in empty, dark classrooms and made love with her. My wife."

It all came back to Reno, in a flood, a maelstrom of memory. William Rennick breathed heavily.

"Sit down, my friend, in the chair across from me. You can set your machine down on the end table."

Rennick sank into the chair, flung his head back and sighed. He propped the machine as Professor Reno had suggested. "You're not my friend," he gasped, staring at the ceiling.

"It was so long ago. Does it even matter now. I was under the impression that you were unable to, unable…"

"I became impotent three years after I married Celeste. Rheumatic fever, something like that. But we loved each other madly, sir."

"I'm sorry," said the professor.

Rennick cleared his throat, took three deep breaths. "I've waited for this moment, you know. I promised myself decades ago to seek you out, but only if something happened to Celeste. And here I am."

He removed a snub-nosed revolver from his coat pocket. "I'm sorry too," he said. "How ironic, we're both dying anyway. Too bad, too bad."

With no flourish, as if it consumed all his strength, he shot Professor Reno in the chest. Reno felt his chair lurch backwards; he tried to claw away the intense pain but it seemed to spread throughout his being like a drop of ink in water. He wiped at the blood and stared at his wet, red fingers.

"Why?" he managed to gasp. "So long ago."

"It has eaten me alive," said Rennick. "Now I can die in peace."

"But…"

"Shhh, save your strength. I knew what was happening all along. I had a friend follow Celeste. And, damn it all, for a while I even loved you for providing what I couldn't. She had no thought of leaving me. Celeste and I were soulmates. You just helped."

Professor Reno felt the coldness first in his feet; it started to rise, seized his groin.

"I'm really dying," he whispered.

"Watch this," Rennick said. He pointed the pistol at his temple and fired. A blast of the man's insides burst from the other side of his head and splattered onto the wall.

He crawled to Rennick's feet and seized the plastic machine. He pulled the tubes out of Rennick's nostrils and inserted them into his own. He struggled back to his own chair and inhaled the oxygen. A terrible, rusty maelstrom roared in his lungs.

He gazed at William Rennick, whose head had drooped slightly forward. Rennick seemed to be smiling. He thought of Celeste, imagined making love with her, for he had never done so, however much he adored her, longed for it. Why had the friend lied? Unless the friend… And slowly, she materialized, and he clutched her flesh, breathed the fragrant bouquet of her delicious hair. He stared into the pale, lifeless eyes of her husband and once more managed to crawl over to him. He pulled himself up across the dead man's lap and passionately kissed his lips. "My angel," he sobbed, "my angel."

Seduction

"Betwixt the trillers of flutes and toilsome tillers," he said—

She could only anticipate, her olive still rocking in its chipped Blue Willow saucer, bereft of pimento, which still, she smacked with ardor, sucking out its redness. She felt a sudden craving for wine, Chardonnay maybe, she who had renounced spirits and not touched a drop in years.

"…March the impeccable, gray-leagued button depressors."

"Whatever are you thinking?" Although she knew because he only thought about one thing, each effusion a variation on the solitary theme. She gazed at the Utrillo print, strangely inappropriate, how sad, she thought. Not that she cared. Nothing matched, not even his socks sometimes. Occasionally she wondered what it would be like to sleep with an executive who wore burgundy ties, starched collars and pin-striped suits. The eyes of executives, though, she remembered, were inertial, like those of fish packed in crushed ice. Eyes of not death exactly, though it was death, but of slate.

"They press little buttons—powder blue buttons, mauve buttons, beige, buttons with no color at all, buttons the color of rainbows, phosphorescent buttons, buttons dead as granite, they press their grainy, oily fingertips onto such buttons and things happen, structures appear, velocities change, dimensions shift, as if… you don't want to hear?"

She squinted at the Utrillo, scanned his bookshelves, inhaled the murky room with its bits of paper strewn everywhere (where did they come from?), molding Oriental—a real Sarouk, he said— from his grandmother—the old furniture with blackening shellac, the bust of Apollo—real marble, he'd said— the mandolin with no strings, the dull pewter candlestick holders, the Indian inkwell—real bronze, he'd said—the brass standing lamp fluting out of which he could never wipe out all the Brasso, the cracked oil painting of a gloating monk, which he'd said had frightened him as a child, the daguerreotype he'd found at a yard sale thinking it was JEB Stuart, the mahogany box hand-carved by his great-grandfather, the Belgian tapestry so worn its figures and color had become one brownish smear, the dead moth somehow still attacked to the ceiling, death glue, he'd said, the Art Nouveau tray for calling cards, he'd said, a practice in the 1890s, when everyone carried a supply of chromo-lithographed messages boarded by Cupids and valentines and roses, with messages like *forget me not* or *don't despair,* silly, he'd said, but something in them anyway, like the one in his tray, over one hundred years old, executed by the great printer Louis Prang, stating simply *rejoice,* yet not cornily religious, they had something then, he said, nothing like the plastic and Styrofoam now, the hasty waste, what with no time, time has accelerated, he'd said, don't you find?, like rain suddenly falling faster, thickening, acquiring density, no longer vapor, diaphanous, but almost like nuggets or tiny shafts, notice how the wind can turn it inside out although the inside of water and the outside are the same, unlike anything else except maybe, he'd said, nitrogen, helium, methane, even diamonds become gas in stars, diamond gas, imagine, or a chunk or solid oxygen, what would it taste like? Slimy or porous or powdery or like metal, doesn't all metal taste the same?

And when she turned, pursed her lips, to address him, realizing he'd been rambling, heard the click outside the window, or clock, like two bricks knocked together, the click or clock they always heard, which at first alarmed until it had happened often enough to become part of the universe, she merely groaned.

"I know you're tired," he said. "I'd give you an aspirin but we're out. No juice either. Only the tap. Sometimes I think women always change, like fire, while men stay the same. Men are like boulders, women fire. It's nature, tragic, ruinous, sublime too… but fatal, for the boulders."

She didn't want to hear any more words. He seemed composed of words; if you picked him apart with delicate tools some words would spill out—*gelatinous, ephebe, blanch, pleached,* words that were unreal, that he'd acquired and stitched into himself—while other words would have to be pried from deeply within spleen and kidneys, the moist, feverish organs, words that had created him because they were alive first, covetous words yearning for form, flesh, words too residual to remember, though she know they were there, lodged within like stakes, pinned with carriage bolts or rivets, immutable… he was right, women were fire, and despite it all, she listened, while longing for something else, more, a different paradigm, to use his word. Gases, molecules, radiation, vectors, probabilities, electromagnetism… something beyond even these, which she knew, mainly from him, did not count, failed to tell the whole story. And there was a story being told.

He'd turned her on to the mystics, trying to get at it. "St. Teresa with her quivering spear," he'd laughed, "which Maria Bonaparte said was nothing more than—" He had trouble with certain words, *penis*. "Don't like it," he'd said, eyes lowered in mock shame, "too, too... clinical? What? Rhymes with Venus, though, handy, eh? The sum of its weight times its cube plus eight is his phone number give him a call. You'd never know I was a Puritan."

Oh yes, she thought. Despite the penchant for gutter terms, which she saw as empty bravado, like the patina on his bronze thingamajig. The world is not made of fire, as he said Heraclitus said, fire is made of the world. She suddenly desired a plump, dewy fig, the kind she'd seen as a kid, growing in her parents' back yard on a thick old, cracked tree. Where he'd said he discovered the secret sin, up on a limb of a fig tree on Wisteria Street, perched in the branches like an owl, hidden by green Spring leaves. Odd, their pasts both contained fig trees. She'd never like figs, nor did he. "Too soggy," he'd said, "a taste like tuberculosis, sickly sweet. And when they rot on the ground, it's beyond nausea. Disgusting mush, fruit flies, decay at its most rank."

Yes, true, but now she wanted to bite into a swollen, ripe fig. There would be no words in a fig, just figness, a tiny pregnancy, the viscous fat congealing with nothing left over, the split of fecundity, fuzzy brownish pulp.

"Let's go to Kroger and get some figs," she said.

He stared, alert, interested. One eye was larger than the other, one round, the other ovoid. Intricate pink ganglia muting the whites. "No figs," he said, "only apples, oranges... we have abandoned the tropics."

And abruptly, with fierce vengeance, she felt the words reveal themselves... *apples, oranges, equatorial tropics...* and understood she had been duped all along, that the only hope, for him as well, for everyone, was mute forgetfulness. "Adam should never have named the animals," she murmured, sinking dreamily into the settee. "A man, naturally."

"Or unnaturally," he said, desire forking through his body like voltage.

"Foreplay," she cooed, "who needs it?"

The Theory of Specific Relativity

His friend, the once eminent but now drunken, catastrophized astro-quantum physicist, has just explained the difference between matter and waves, or rather, something and nothing. Not his friend. They just happened to meet in a shoddy little bar called El Greco on Burgundy St., a narrow, dark street in the Vieux Carre where people get killed.

They sit slumped over the bar, talking, mumbling; they sit erectly in wicker rockers in a plush hotel in Belize, overlooking the clear emerald waters of the Gulf. Or in his mother's kitchen, sipping café au lait, he and his friend, a stranger… Jude, is that his name? Once a renowned scientist addressing congressional bodies on the ramifications of nuclear proliferation. Think tank grants, research, stellar success. They slouch in two stiff seats at a theater called the Rivoli—this was decades ago—and watch a movie called "The Vikings." Jude or Henry, his name is probably Henry, says that dense vibrations of waves create matter. Matter is just waves shaken up like a can of paint in one of those machines at Lowe's.

They sit in the cafeteria on wooden chairs eating the hot lunch of the day. Mashed potatoes, meat loaf, green peas, bread pudding for dessert. He doesn't know Henry yet. Henry comes years later. Drunken, mournful Henry. His friend. Just a guy me meets who says that waves become matter when we look at them or touch them or eat them. It's called, Jude wags a finger, the collapse of the wave function.

Henry says ultimate reality is the void, a still yet shimmering void. Something sets it astir, a fly buzzing across the room, the twitch of an aphid. The agitated void we call waves. Speedy, dense waves generate particles. Particles become rocks and flowers and animals and of course us. Or the Tower of Babel. We are, Henry laughs as they sit erectly on the church pew inside St. Louis Basilica, nothing moving fast.

How can that be? he asks his friend, the guy he's just met, some prestigious scholar once but now a remnant of his former self who bleeds from various spots of his body. His pores. Pores, tiny voids of the flesh. His friend is obviously dying. Acute alcohol toxicity.

He sits on a metal chair beside Henry's hospital bed and pats his wrist. How can that be? You're saying we're nothing? I feel the bones of your knuckles. Bones are nothing, my fingers are nothing? Henry smiles, chuckles, it's all in the math. And spirit, don't forget spirit, it's as the Buddhists say.

They sit at a café table in Paris and watch two young women pass in tight blue jeans. No bras. Their breasts bounce slightly, their nipples are erect. This is nothing? Nipples are void? My friend, Henry says, don't try to understand. You can't. I can't, and I'm the expert. Yes, nipples are void but delicious void. Your lips are void, your lips meeting nipples are void, void meets void at different vibratory rates. It's too much to grasp so become a Buddhist and float along an easier path. Though that's not so easy either. Try kundalini. Your brain explodes in an orgasm of delight. I have given up thought as an aberration of existence. Like Lao Tzu, I shall soon ride out of history on an ass.

They sit in a plush brass and oak office. Jude or Henry or whoever he is gives advice on the impending divorce. His friend is a lawyer. They just met. They sit drinking whisky at the El Greco as the theme from "Zorba the Greek" blasts from an ancient jukebox. An obese old woman twirls slowly about the room. Void in motion.

Jude explains to him that she has a right to half his estate and will, assume it as a given, receive custody of the two children. This is the way it goes, Jude sighs, been through it myself, and I'm a lawyer.

They sit in cushiony seats on a jet to Belize. They drink martinis and josh with the stewardess, a blond with glaring scarlet lipstick. Her nipples sneak through her tight blouse. The insatiable urge to touch.

But, he says.

It's all illusion anyway, says Henry. Emanations in and out of nothing. Your little drama, however scathing to the immediate you, the illusion of you, in and out of nothing, which is the only eternal. Where is Rome? The Hittites? Where is Lope de Vega? Where is Ur? Constantine the Great? Socrates? Where are we?

We are clanking in a streetcar up St. Charles Avenue on the way to Camellia Grill for turkey omelets. His friend jokes, OHM-lets. We are gagging in the infernally hot chapel of the International Shrine of St. Jude on Rampart Street. The hopeless have tacked up tiny golden replicas of kidneys, lungs, spleen and every other part of the illusory, astral body onto the plaster walls.

Miracles must occur. When the laws of physics go askew, when the waves oscillate a little faster or slower than they should, when we catch of glimpse of them and they ossify. My friend Henry wants to tack his bloodstream onto the wall but has to settle for a few modest smears of it. He looks at the blood and smiles, I was here. In another sense, he adds, I wasn't here. We have never arrived. I pound on the wall with my fist. This wall is here, now, I cry, here, now.

We are leaning on the rail atop the Empire State Building and I explain that I have just as much right to custody of my daughter as the ex-wife. I begin to cry. I have not seen my daughter in over two years. I appeared in court over thirty-five times and the lawyers defeated me. One of the lawyers is banging the ex-wife, her payment of flesh. Flesh that is nothing. Waves actualized. I didn't have a chance, not with a system of shysters who look out for one another.

My friend pats me on the shoulder, sighs, shakes his head. I've been there, he says. Remember those slushy hot meat ball sandwiches at Joey's on Magazine Street. That's what you need. Go to Joey's, order a meatball sandwich—get them to add some Romano cheese—and sit at the bar, buttocks firmly secured on the stool, eat, and enjoy. Just enjoy. I do not deny the expedience of random joy. Meatball sandwiches saved my life back then, though, of course, it's no guarantee for the future. Look at me.

Blood now seeps from his tear ducts. Watery pink effusions, but blood nevertheless. He tells me the latest theory is strings, although he hasn't kept up. The universe is a banjo. The strings vibrate in harmonic unison. They stretch across all of the void. There is no void. Music, the new waves. The universe is a song, a symphony, maybe an opera. The trick is to perk your ears and sing along.

I'm too busy for music, I say as we slouch upon two rocks in Armenia. This is a tragic place. Women in black veils everywhere you turn, in mourning. Evil, sad things have happened here. I hear a duduka in the distance, he says. Plaintive, melancholic, so beautiful you want to die.

My friend, the gifted historian, has overlooked Armenia in his sweeping assessments of the world. It doesn't figure, he says, like the massless neutrinos that streak out of the sun and pass right through us, our bodies, the entire planet, and head for the other edge of the universe. For what reason? Armenia, a gravely massive neutrino, with no destination.

Of course, you could say the same of Uruguay, Portugal, Arkansas.

Of course, you can say anything about anything. You could say two wrongs don't make a right, or two rights don't make a wrong, or there is no right, only three wrongs. This is why I have dismissed expertise. I notice the blood trickle from his ears. He wears two ruby pierced earrings. Drops of blood.

You are bleeding to death, I tell my friend. Why can't they do something?

We are ovaling up the jagged hairpin turns of Pike's Peak. We want an overview.

We linger in El Greco, order more ouzo. I don't drink ouzo, I laugh. Henry runs up the tab. In my capacity, he clears his throat, I have advised presidents. Imagine. Kennedy. The man was in constant pain and yet he pursued new women each day. Fucked them in broom closets, limousines, bathrooms... anywhere. It's as if testosterone has a life of its own and merely uses us as vehicles of transport. It was a woman who brought me down, friend, to my present condition. I lost my reputation, my family, my fortune.

Glad to meet you, call me Jude. And you are?

We stroll over to Café du Monde for beignets. Jude wheezes, can hardly make it; he has to take my arm. And what's your story? he asks. Don't tell me, I know your story. It's Everystory. Did you know that sub-atomic particles, once in contact, can zip toward extreme ends of the cosmos and in defiance of the mandatory rigors of the speed of light, can communicate. Tickle one over on the left, the one on the right laughs. Instantly. Bell's Theorem. Faster than light. This is a non-local affair. We're all connected.

I smirk. I am no longer connected to my children. They have been abducted. You can't use that word in court, my lawyer friend insists, they will adjudge you fanatical, unstable. But it's the truth! I say. Henry swills another ouzo. The truth, he says, is virtual. It pops in and out of existence at its own pace. You must dress conservatively, speak softly and appeal for mercy. Do you love your children?

I find it degrading to appeal for mercy from brigands.

We mosey over to the riverfront and take a bench beside a troupe of mimes. The mimes pretend to be moving but remain fixed in place. They have white faces, clown faces, heavy mascara and painted red lips. The river currents move in waves. The river is matter. I have reached the end of my line, says my new friend Jude, or should I say string? There's a wonderful little story called "A Piece of String." It ends tragically, and all because a peasant found a piece of string in a field and put it in his pocket. You never know what will trip you up. We like to think it's the big stuff, women, children, family... but I suspect it's something more fundamental, and pathetic. I watch as a nurse adjusts Henry's IV. A plastic sack of liquid nutrients, drip, drip, drip. He phases in and out of consciousness.

Comrade, he whispers, I have succumbed to the poison. Like Socrates long ago. Except I was never as smart or principled. Just on to a little something along the road. Something I spotted, a piece of string or glitter perhaps, a sequin. And I rode on it like a flying saucer until Beatrice. Such a name, eh? Undone, undone by nipples defying a blouse. Do you realize that all men are Oriental despots by nature?

My friend is now awash in his own blood. Waves of blood. I hardly got to know ye, he says, but we conjoined at some minor interstice in spacetime, assemblages of sub-atomic particles reuniting after long separation. It's a local affair.

We are sitting in Café Reggio in the Village listening to some poet read an epic-length poem about his own personal doom. We drift to City Lights Bookstore across the continent, where I once lost a contact lens. I rub my fingers across the floor and find it, a dehydrated, shriveled speck of matter. Fifteen years! I cry.

We are Walking the streets of Istanbul, Cairo, Jerusalem. Someone sells apples from a wheelbarrow. A peasant who does not know or care that reality is illusory. I bite into the apple. It is crisp, tart and juicy. It contains, of course, a worm.

My friend, whose name I never caught, though Henry rings a bell, dies as I hold his hand. There ensues a great flurry among the nurses. A doctor finally rushes in to declare it official. Henry's children cannot be located. They want nothing to do with him.

I don't count, I just met the man in a bar, see?

Bikers flood into the El Greco. I sit alone at a table sipping ouzo. One of the bikers borrows a chair. Doing ok, cap'n? he asks. I must look a sight, a mime, an Armenian refugee. Name's Frank, he says and offers to shake. Call me Jude, I say. St. Jude, Frank laughs, I know him. Are you a hopeless case?

The question startles me, I shake my head, adjust to what I think is reality at the moment. No, I say, I'm getting over something. My kids, you see...

Frank pulls up the chair he borrowed. Let me tell you, he says as he signals a waitress with, no doubt, taut nipples drifting out of her blouse or t-shirt. Little bullets of flesh. Composed of atoms, mostly void.

Yep, he says, something's terribly wrong. How do you think I wound up on a motorcycle? Maybe you should see a doctor. I think your nose is bleeding.

No, I say, just some leftovers from this guy I knew. It rubs off. This guy, do you know what he said? That we're nothing, just vibrations that harden into something you can recognize.

Yeah? Frank says. Guess that's why I'm so jittery, eh? Loose parts.

No, I say. That guy went too far. Killed him. I'm going to leave now and go beg for mercy. No, not beg. I'm going to request mercy. Don't ever know too much, Frank. It clouds the issue.

Frank finds this extraordinarily funny and spasms in laughter as I leave the table. Don't worry, he cries after me, that was never an option. Hell, I don't even know who I am.

Frank, man, that's just a name I plucked out of the air. Me? I could be anybody. Even you. You know what they say…

I plug my ears with my fingers and rush out into the teeming, glistening, unending streets.

Mind emerges out of wet, slushy gray matter with circuitry. I do not mind that mind is nothing. No thing. I dream of children. Tickle the one on the right, the one on the left giggles.

The Last Mosquito

All summer I'd fought them with DEET, swatters, citronella candles and electronic traps. Now I only wanted to sit out on the deck and enjoy the sun and late beauty of fall without being attacked. Is that too much to ask? I remain Buddhistic about harming any of God's creatures, but the onslaught had gone on too long and too relentlessly. And I'm allergic to the infidels. They leave throbbing welts and destroy peace of mind and I itch until scratching myself raw. Who knows what infections they harbor? And of course the diseases.

It seems, according to Encylopedia.Com, that the only purpose mosquitoes serve is to provide bats with food. This, given the ravages they have always inflicted upon the world, seems not good enough, not in my book. Surely bats could subsist on gnats, fruit flies and a host of other swarming things.

Hence, my plan to go on a rampage, cause minor mayhem in the ecological balance.

The circumstances:

Mid-October, Indian summer. (Should that be native American summer?) A fabulous day, the yard layered with red, purple, ocher, orange leaves. Weather you had to be out in.

Two months earlier I'd thrown out my lower back and suffered excruciating pain and near paralysis for a week. Then a regimen of chiropractors and physical therapists. A month later a whole-body systemic rash spreads like California wildfires across my entire body. It oozes, scales, itches, lays me low until the prednisone, which begets its own problems. So I'd had it with misery. Like stepping into the book of Job except I'm not patient. I tend to binge on rage.

So one particular day I'm out in sublimely gorgeous nature, sitting on my deck chair, propped up on a lumbar support pillow, still nursing the evil rash. And beside me a Smith & Wesson .38 caliber snub-nosed revolver. Don't worry, no suicidal thoughts from this wretch. But earlier I'd heard one lone mosquito violining in the area, and I knew it would head straight for me if I tried to enjoy the afternoon. Remember, not many more days like this. Soon winter will beset us.

I sit, take in the climate voraciously, the birdsong, the golden leaves, the ratcheting of squirrels... I meditate, maybe pray... but mostly enjoy. And then the infernal hum near my left ear. I swat, miss, the mosquito vortexes away.

This is surely the last one of the season. One great advantage of winter: it destroys the furies. But it's unseasonably warm today. Thus my mission to blast the last foe into Valhalla in a fiery, apocalyptic, Viking blast the moment it rests somewhere other than on my body. Demented, enraged, I want revenge. I think of the torque, vector and sheer power of the slug as it zooms toward the enemy like an asteroid, makes contact, takes its victim for a short ride toward Armageddon.

So when it finally lights atop the book on my deck table, I slowly lift the pistol and even more slowly stand and back away a few paces to take aim... ah, the moment of truth, Judgment Day, Cosmic Justice, Kairos, Apotheosis!

I gaze at my adversary... he looks even more pathetic than I with my leprous rash. An old mosquito bereft a leg, a ripped wing, hungry, lonely, the last of his kind for the year. And my finger on the trigger, the fingers of my other hand gripped around my wrist...

And lower the gun. I can't do it. I cannot slay my enemy. Sure, I'd killed many during the summer, but only in self-defense as they besieged me. But this was premeditated murder. All God's creatures.

And could the mosquito help being a mosquito? Think of its previous lives, the ultra-bad Karma coming back in such fashion, detested by everyone on the planet. I believe the great poet D.H Lawrence once wrote a poem about mosquitoes, in which he declares that they suck blood out of need, which is better and more moral than plutocrats hoarding money in the bank. Yeah, he said that... and I agree.

So I didn't shoot the mosquito, I didn't shoot myself, I didn't shoot anything. I sat down in my chair, picked up the book, the mosquito came near, sniffed, and staggered slowly away. Maybe the rash repelled it, but I like to think some kind of transaction or communion occurred, some mysterious bond. Stupid, I know, but since when is wise ever very wise?

Watermelon Spit

In those days we kids played with rocks and sticks we found in the street, battered pinecones from old Miss Yunt's yard, bits of dusty twine, dented tin cans we plucked out of trash cans. The greatest treat was an appliance box abandoned on some curb. The newest ones smelled so caustic they burned our eyes, especially when we carved out little windows and doors with pocketknives and released the corrugated gases binding layers of stiff, chemically treated paper. But this is not a story about poverty and cardboard boxes; this is a story of revenge most heinous.

Meet the villains, my cousin Jackie and me. Jackie wore a clunky hearing aid amplifier on his chest with a wire and phone plug running up to his left ear. He was two years older, wiry, fast and fearless. Jackie would take on any odds and I often used him to do our dirty work since his devotion to me was unwavering. I feared physical violence more than the polio germs our parents whispered about, more than the evil communists and A-bombs. I think Jackie felt so loyal because I alone in the neighborhood understood his garbled tongue. The deafness had mangled his speech; he had stopped hearing much, when right before he was born, his mother came down with German measles. Jackie would do anything I asked; I could have made him my slave. Rumors of his impossible strength and ferocity hummed through the streets and alleyways, clacked with the swaying bamboo stalks in Uncle Achille's backyard. No kid, unless totally ignorant or insane, would dare mess with my cousin.

Two or three blocks away there lived a much older boy, I'm guessing now around eighteen, but he was so massive, so obese and blobish, he could have been twenty-five for all we knew, an actual man and not a boy at all. Other kids called him "Ernest," but we had our own name for this behemoth. Watermelon. Oh, he hated that name. We had no mercy. We taunted him whenever he hobbled past the house on his way to the bus stop, which was just about every day. "Hey, Watermelon," we would cry, "when are they going to eat you? You're about to explode!" Or Jackie, in his mangled way, might zigzag around him in a frantic little dance, screeching, "Wa-meln, Wa-meln, Wa-meln!" Watermelon would swipe at him, stretch out his blubbery arms and fingers, which looked like pale sausages, and try to grab him by the shirt collars, but Jackie always dashed away. Anyone was too fast for Watermelon, maybe even slug were too fast.

The boy or man or whatever just seemed to sway along, a human boulder, the momentum of his weight propelling him forward. When he reached the bus stop, a concrete pole embedded in the mud, he leaned against it, kicked at the broken shells beneath his feet. We heard he rode up Miro Street to Esplanade, then transferred all the way to the statue of Mother Cabrini near City park. He kneeled before that statue and prayed for hours. That's what we heard.

Watermelon never spoke to us or screamed or cursed when we attacked him, never talked back or gave us any lip, but he smirked, looked at us poisonously and smirked. That smirk drove us wild. We wanted to wipe it off his face. We were barbarous, I guess, though not a little afraid. But we trusted our speed, our energy and our knowledge of every path of escape, however intricate, in the block. It was unthinkable that Watermelon would ever catch us.

How we loved those gigantic appliance boxes. We scouted the streets, lugged them back to our sidewalk, jabbed at them with our knives, constructed outer space stations, forts, castles, club houses. Only rain thwarted our plans. One summer shower could melt those boxes into flat, brown, gooey jelly that our parents made us shovel off the banquet. So whenever we found a box, we had to work fast, waste no time. A box meant instant gratification. And we shot our sisters with water guns from the windows. Sometimes they threw rocks at the boxes, but we just laughed. It felt good inside, especially when the sun smeared them with heat, and the heat made us sleepy. So we spent a lot of time just sleeping, right there on the sidewalk, as people came and went. In those days all kinds of people just roamed around. They didn't have anything else to do. Sometimes a stray cat would push in the cardboard flap of a door and curl up with us. That was nice.

Well, one day a ferocious jolting instantly roused us from our snooze. The entire box quaked from side to side; we thought it was an earthquake the way it flung our bodies around. Then the box started to turn over on itself; we rolled with it for about twenty yards. Jackie's elbow nearly poked out one of my eyes. Our skulls clacked more than once. When the box stopped moving, we shuddered in fear and wondered if we should try to dash out of the carved door. Before we could decide, the box began to boom from every side as if someone were beating it with a baseball bat. One of the thwacks caught me in the spine and would leave a bruise for weeks to come.

In that particular box we had carved a skylight. Slowly, ever so slowly, something was poking down the cardboard flap of that skylight. Jackie and I flattened ourselves at the bottom, cringed and awaited our fate not like good soldiers or tough cowpokes, but mewling little girls. And finally, when the skylight flap was fully distended, what should we behold but the monstrous, rapturous, sweaty, blood-flushed face of a crazed Watermelon! He stared at us, cackled, punched the sides of the box some more, growled and hissed like an animal. His breath flooded the box like a poisonous cloud. It smelled like manure the ragman's horse dropped in the street. We were doomed. There was no hope of escape.

And then the worst. Watermelon pursed his lips, sucked down what must have been gallons of snot from his sinuses, and gave us that smirk. His lips parted and putrid phlegm rained down on us, on our faces and clothes, in our hair. One mouthful of rotten phlegm and mucous after another. It seethed with worms and maggots, seaweed, chunks of fat, gristle, dead minnows and goldfish, toothpicks, chewing tobacco, fish bones, coffee grounds, scorpions and human teeth. A maelstrom of disgusting filth from inside Watermelon's body. Jackie and I prepared to drown and repeated the Hail Mary frantically. But suddenly, abruptly as the siege had begun, it ended. Watermelon's face disappeared. He kicked the box one last time and hobbled on to the bus stop. We poked our heads out of the skylight and watched him cross the street. We screamed, cursed and threatened to kill him, burn his house down, chop him into little pieces with PaPaw's ax. He leaned against the bus stop pole, smirked and gave us the bird.

By this point we were hysterical and coated with slime. We crawled out of the box and rushed into our separate houses, which amounted to different sides of the same house that had been divided down the middle by the landlord. I flew through living room, bedroom, hallway, back to the kitchen, where I knew I would find my mother ironing. I sobbed shamelessly in the doorway. Mom dropped the iron onto the linoleum floor, quickly picked it up and turned it off. She dragged me to the bathroom, tore off my clothes and rubbed me down with one wet towel after another. She rubbed Dr. Tichenor's Antiseptic into every pore of my skin. Some of it splashed into my eyes and I cried out in pain. Mom didn't say a word as she toiled. But I screamed and whimpered, coughed, howled, cursed Watermelon and his fetid phlegm, vowed revenge and mayhem. Mom wrapped me in a towel and led me to the sofa. I spread out on it, my head in her lap. She stroked my hair and hummed her favorite song, which always soothed me. "Apple Blossom Time."

And now, dumbfounded over the passage of so many decades, the tidal crest of time since the incident on Columbus Street, I am only beginning to understand that Watermelon let Jackie and me off pretty easy. He could have hurt us badly. He could have heaved himself onto the box and crushed us to death. He could have stoned us, stabbed us with sticks, wrenched up our arms and legs and snapped them in two. Instead, he showered us with spit and snot, which washed off easily enough. Of course we felt ashamed of ourselves; we had hounded him relentlessly. We were mean-spirited savages.

Yet Watermelon, our enemy, had bestowed a kind of mercy on us. Jackie and I continued to plot against him, made plans to assail him with stones next time he passed, but our hearts weren't in it. A part of us got thrown out with that box. And oddest of all, we never saw Watermelon again. He simply disappeared from the neighborhood. But that's what happened in those days, people just disappeared, and no one ever asked any questions. Or someone new would show up and you had to wait a while to see what would come of it. A few years later Jackie and I disappeared too when we moved away from Columbus Street. Not so long ago, seized with nostalgia, I drove past the old house, but it too had vanished, bull-dozed out of existence to make way for a low-income day care center. I spotted in the rear view, as I made my exit, some boys in the street swinging sticks and hurling rocks at a stop sign. One of them looked pretty familiar.

LeBruchio & Father, Movers

My wife and I had finally packed all the books and china and doodads and linens and utensils and tools... what a load it all made: boxes taped and sealed stacked high throughout the rooms, all the furniture disassembled and ready to go. We wanted to be frugal and did all the packing ourselves, but we both had had it with the actual transferring of a household into a truck and then lugging it all back in to the new place. So we found this outfit in the yellow pages, Lebruchio & Father, which, I swear we had used years earlier as Lebruchio & Son.

When they showed up, two hours late, a massive, smiling man stood outside the door.

We shook hands and he asked if he could look around, get a handle on the situation. I noticed a frail old man following Lebruchio, the father I presumed, who after all the years had traded places with his son, he now the ancillary. This is what age does—the child is father of the man and all that. The father looked so ravaged by time, the wife and I could only guess that Son wanted to make him feel useful. Those old ones really need to feel useful, don't ask me why. I will personally find nothing appealing about usefulness and hope when I become wretched and infirm. I pray no one will want to use me for anything.

So Lebruchio, a gentle giant, got to work and hoisted appliances onto a dolly, wasting no time. The father followed meekly along, carrying out a box of tissues here, some shirts on hangers there. Painful to watch. At one point he hobbled over to the wife and, after coughing and hacking, asked her if she had anything else light he could haul. She handed him her comb and a toothbrush. He shook his head and signed, "One at a time, I'll be back for the comb." He trotted out with the toothbrush and slipped it into the pocket of Lebruchio Younger who was now in the process of carrying out three large boxes of hardbacks all at once.

When it was all done the wife and I lowered ourselves onto the floor and stretched out. After all, we had worked hard too—any move is hard work, even if you're watching. Then we heard the weeping. I followed it to a back room and found Lebruchio, Sr., huddled in a corner, whimpering and rubbing his eyes. "He's forgotten me again," he gasped, and my knee has given out. I can't make it to the truck. He's about to pull out." Well, I scooped up the old man in my arms and carried him through the house, out the front door and signaled Lebruchio, ready to depart. He opened the shotgun door and I slid in the old man, who still wept. "Sorry about that," Lebruchio laughed. They just don't know when to quit, do they?" I raised my eyebrows, slipped him an envelope of money. He removed a twenty and passed it back to me— "For moving my father," he sighed.

Piano Lessons

Parents ever tell you "It may seem like hell now but you'll be thankful later, believe us?"

And of course, now that it is later, you're thankful, sure, you can play all those etudes, mazurkas and polonaises by Chopin and Bach's fierce toccata.

Your friend, Kayla, can't.

You, unlike Kayla, have a skill, a talent, a resume boost.

Poor Kayla, while you were practicing chaotic arpeggios, she was out getting trashed for Mardi Gras.

Poor, Kayla, no F-sharp minors, no key signatures, no chromatic scales, no Chopin, no Bach.

And what does she have to show for all that jazz save the baby?

Bricks

He slid into shotgun effortlessly, smoothly, as I idled at a red light with closed eyes listening to Yo-Yo Ma stroke the cello to Brahms's Double Concerto. I didn't even realize he was there until he cleared his throat.

"What kind of shit you listen," he spat, droplets of spit splattering the dash.

I whipped my head around to confront one wreck of a man— grizzled, about fifty, sunbaked, disheveled, haunted.

"Hey," I cried, "out my car, you!"

He looked at me with watery eyes and a compassionate smile. I noticed the revolver he clutched in one hand and stroked with the other, oddly to the precise movements of YoYo's bow.

"Maybe it ain't so bad. What kind of music is that?"

Stunned by the pistol and now shaking, I asked, "What do you want?"

"Better drive on," he said. "Light green now. Just drive and I will let you live."

"Let me live?" I sputtered, choking on the words.

I noted that he had pivoted the pistol toward me, target: upper rib cage.

"I've never asked much of my fellow man," he said. "But my beloved son Kenny is in trouble bad and needs me. You just drive and I will let you live. What's your line of work? I see a white shirt, pressed pants and an untied necktie. A desk man."

"I'm a claims adjuster for Allstate. I'm late to work. My office is just up the street. Can I at least run in and tell them I'll be coming back?"

"First thing, man, never assume I'm stupid. Just drive. I laid bricks in my time. Honest work. You the guy who tells people you won't cover their damages. I understand but deplore. Bet you never laid a brick in your papery life. You just write things down in a ledger or something."

"Where are we going?" I felt droplets of sweat drip from my armpits. How could this be happening?

"You follow Main Street here until it turns into Highway 11 and

Louis Gallo

bring me over to

Bakersville. Kenny lives there in the first trailer park. He's hurt. And by the way I'll need your wallet too—for insurance. I am not a thief. You'll get it back. Reach in your pocket real slow and hand it to me. Kenny had such a good heart but things didn't work out for him. I understand everything. Them with good hearts go down first. Can't compete with the evil."

Strange to say, I almost felt some sympathy for my abductor. I can read people. I know when customers are lying. I'd lay money that this ruin of a man wasn't lying.

"Then you'll let me go? You won't shoot me? And return my wallet?"

"Yep, though you'll get the wallet in the mail. As I said, insurance. You understand, right? You're in that business. Now you see what it feels like when you screw them over."

"I don't screw them over. I assess damages and causes. People lie. They try to defraud insurance companies all the time."

"I seen your insurance buildings. Skyscrapers, a lot on them. Glass and brass. Who does the screwing—or defrauding to use your word? We live with it, the theft, but you don't. You want more and more and more and don't care who gets crushed in the process. Kenny don't have insurance, so I might have to borrow your credit card in case we need a doctor. He tried to hang himself. The landlord happened to hear a crash since he was nearby carrying out some trash bags. The trailer door was open. He found Kenny thrashing with the noose around his neck and pulled him down, then called me. You just comply for the time being and you be ok."

"Comply," I growled boldly, plotting out how I might disarm the man and throw him out of the car. He seemed a soft touch despite the gun. What was I thinking? I don't know the first thing about self-defense or how to disarm someone. The very word *disarm* smacks of horror.

So I did indeed comply and as we headed for a trailer park in Bakersville my abductor leaned his head against the rest and closed his eyes. But he warned, "Just because I have closed eyes doesn't mean I can't see you. Beware. And play that music again. What is it? I never heard anything like that."

****

I received my wallet in a crumpled envelop a few days later. It contained a note:

Kenny needed x-rays but is ok, mostly skin burns from the rope. We went to Urgent Care to save you some money. You had enough cash to cover it—seven hundred dollars. Who has that much cash in their wallets? Got your address from one of your business cards. Soon I will pay you back in kind, not money. Who has money? If we could afford insurance it would not have cost you much. Build yourself a barbeque. Get your hands dirty. The gun wasn't loaded. Forgive me.

The next week I heard a loud noise out back and went to check. Some men were unloading thousands of bricks from a truck and tossing them into the yard in chaotic fashion. I tried to protest but the head guy intervened, told me to "back off." He didn't seem the kind of person susceptible to reason.

It must have been at least two tons of bricks, a massive mound—which I assumed amounted to seven hundred dollars' worth. My abductor was true to his word.

I approached the edge of the pile and grasped a brick. Gritty it was and obviously used before. And heavier than it looked.

I drove over to Lowe's and bought a few bags of mortar. But I wouldn't be building a barbeque pit.

Legs

When they cut off my Uncle Henry's legs I was off smoking weed with a girl who said she was the great-great-great niece of President William Henry Harrison, the one who never made it to the White House. I remember an efficiency rank with cat piss and stale Purina, a green cotton spread on the mattress, Southern Comfort, vanilla candles, and Jim Morrison in the background, her favorite, though I inclined toward Jackie Wilson or Ben E. King. I'd hate to think we reached the sublime right as that blade dug into my uncle's bones. It must have smelled grisly like when dentist's drill into some sick molar.

He was a big man who would capture you at reunions and boom the secrets of direct marketing, mail order and free advertising into your face. My cousins and I tried not to meet his eye, but he always cornered Sandy because at the time she had those new breasts which he always managed to brush against. Back then it disgusted us, though now I think I understand; I was out trying to do the same thing, not with Sandy, although she too crossed my mind. He just seemed so old and his teeth had turned into kernels of corn. He had a wife, of course, my mother's sister, but aunts and mothers don't figure when it comes to love you can call love.

The decline began when a drunk broadsided Uncle's van and they had to pry him out with crowbars and two-by fours. A miracle he survived, everybody said. Broken ribs, two crushed legs, spleen damage—there's more, always more, but at some point you lose count. We saw him a few times buzzing around in a wheelchair with two massive casts on his legs. The doctors discovered diabetes during their probe and that's what finally ruined him, not the accident. His skin started to swell and blacken and gangrene set in long after the broken bones had mended.

Years later I saw him out at his ranch-style house in Picayune, where my family and I drove for a mercy visit—even I dimly aware that a finale had commenced. He slumped in the same wheelchair with a green shawl hiding the missing legs. He didn't talk much anymore but sometimes he'd laugh at a joke or groan. Aunt Ruth said he had high fever all the time and felt horrible. He no longer tried to corner anybody and his voice had shriveled to distant static. He didn't even notice Sandy, who'd come along for the ride. I saw him pick at a tray of cheese cubes stabbed with party toothpicks. Mostly, he sat in the corner and stared at some game show on television.

Before the funeral I had too much to drink. My sister, cousins and I clumped together in a vestibule. I'd brought along a new girlfriend who smirked a lot as we made snotty comments about relatives we hated. Everyone wore black except us—we planned to invade the French Quarter soon as we could slip away from the wake. My mother had dragged me over to the casket to take a last look at the man who once spent an entire day locating a suitcase of mine; the railroad has lost it on my trip to New Jersey, where Uncle and his family lived before he retired back home to the south. It was easy and free staying with them while I spent my days and most of the nights prowling Manhattan. I never thanked my uncle for his trouble.

We headed straight for Bourbon Street. My cousins and sister disappeared soon enough and I wound up in Lafitte's Blacksmith shop with Wanda, who smoked two cigarettes at once, white fangs dangling from the meat of her glossy violet lip. I drank vodka martinis until all the shitty things she said about life, love, politics, men and God shrank into the screech of some pitiful insect. But, God, she had gorgeous legs, chiseled, they seemed, right out of a vat of Coppertone. Someone started to plunk "I'm Walking" on the bar piano and patrons gathered round to sing. Dimly, I heard Wanda call my uncle a pig. It was my fault. I'd told her all the stories. But just then I felt pretty sorry for him. "You don't know one God-damned thing," I growled as the room spun. When I stood up to leave my knees quivered and I knew I was headed straight down before I got anywhere, faster than that dumb president who missed the White House or an old man with no legs.

Spoon?

I'm trying to repair the light fixture that dangles from the ceiling of my mother's back shed. I am here on vacation, visiting what little Katrina left of the city and what few relatives and friends remain—and trying to help out my mother by taking on chores long overdue. I arrive each year in June and am always stunned at how a mere twelve moons changes reality.

My mother can hardly get around with two canes or a walker now. Her dowager's hump has nearly bent her in half. I try not to notice, I try to remember better days… but.

This year we have a surprise visitor, my mother's sister, Aunt Leah, who is ninety-six years old. I haven't seen her in a decade and didn't recognize her at first. Oh, the degradations. She has shriveled to half her size, speaks in a cartoon rasp and she too requires a walker. My mother says that her children kicked her out of the house in Picayune after a spat, and Mom drove all the way to Mississippi to collect her, Mom, who can hardly walk. Talk about the blind leading the blind.

Anyway, I have unscrewed the filthy, greasy bulb from its socket and need a new seventy-five watt to test if the fixture is getting juice. I return to the house to find Mom and Aunt Leah slouched over the kitchen table with bowls of fresh figs, oatmeal and two steaming cups of Community Coffee with chicory. The fluorescent light has gone dim and buzzes erratically. Exactly when did age undo them both? I can't pinpoint the moment. I don't recall them as wizened crones, and I expect them to emerge rejuvenated at any moment. As they were. As we all were. Who goes unscathed?

My good friend Pierre in Virginia groans that whenever he peers into the mirror he beholds Colonel Khadafi. When I so peer, I see a shadowy, desolate Nosferatu.

"Hi, Jake," Mom laughs, still chipper despite it all. "Want some coffee. Just made it."

"Mom, do you have a light bulb? So I can tell if it's the bulb or fixture that's bad. Well, I know the old bulb is bad."

Both women wear shapeless cotton shifts that drape loosely over their bones.

My mother cocks an ear. "Ehhhhh?" she says? She is also going deaf and sleeps in a rocker before the television set, the volume up to max. My guest bedroom is upstairs and sometimes I hear "The Star-Spangled Banner" blasting through the house as a station signs off for the night.

Aunt Leah looks startled, the way really old people often do. She slowly raises her thin, tissued, onion-skinned arm towards me, a kitchen utensil pinched between her fingers. "Need a spoon?" she croaks?

Globs of slimy oatmeal drip onto the linoleum floor.

Should I laugh or cry as it suddenly dawns on me that no one in this whole freaking world ever really needs a seventy-five-watt light bulb much less a gooey spoon, that everything is broken and askew and beyond repair. And worse–or better, it doesn't matter.

Jonathan Edwards

E dwards rises at four a.m., a gaunt, fearsome figure, feeling his way along the walls through darkness, his long spidery fingers electrified by the dense evil saturating the very atoms of all matter. He studies thirteen hours a day without fail and has thoroughly demoralized the colony. The desperate congregation finally oust him. How can they endure the fruit of such wisdom, their suspension over the pit of Hell by mere gossamer? In the end it is he alone who bears the full extent of mankind's depravity. We say, then, that he represents one pole of the evolving American mind. But this pole, does it not also signify something unsound, a fissure, actually a wound in the intellect it is said to represent? There was too much weeping on those long walks into the howling wilderness, during which he lured his beloved savior to ravish him. There in that dusty clearing, when it happened, we see Edwards writhing on the ground, foaming, screaming with ecstasy as Our Lord penetrates. Afterwards, all is gloom again.

"Infinite upon infinite, infinite upon infinite," we hear him mumble, imagining him hunched in his somber clothing, pacing the room, hands affixed to his sides–the actor Max von Sydow would do a good job with this–muttering, "infinite upon infinite," knowing that his wickedness increases without absolution, that to assuage God, he must fling himself below Hell. This, at least, he had spared his congregation. Hell–a mere rap on the knuckles, a picture in the storybook.

He takes time off from his consuming project, the salvation of his soul, to sire five children (was himself the only boy among ten adoring sisters). These few moments set aside, does therein lie his sin? To have enjoyed the flesh of a woman for its own sake? Or does it go deeper, this self-confessed yet hidden flaw in his soul? Pride. Well, yes, he admits as much. And what was he up to as a young man when he and his comrades trekked into the woods to pray? Pray or play, or was pray player and thus poisoned at the outset? Could any of this have spawned such seething self-hatred and constant yearning for annihilation? Note his obsession with the word *sweet* in the *Personal Narrative*, his unfinished opus of monumental grief. Except, of course, when he is no longer himself, when he has been graced with reprieve. All is darkness, gloom, harrowing when he returns. His heaven, let us not deny it, is boring–a beauteous, perfect, tranquil, peace, yet here he aspires.

What unrelieved tension, what conflict of body and soul, what inner explosion of infinite upon infinite can explain this hunger for holy calmness in all things, to sing God's praises without cease, to proclaim the heinous doctrine of predestination as just or delightful? And then he could turn on you, dangle you over a black chasm, condemn your soul eternally... apply the terror with eloquence. He stands before us at the pulpit, shrouded in black, never moving his body, gazing infinitely into our souls never changing the tone of his voice, creating the spider, becoming the spider, constructing the web, breathing the fire. We shrink into ourselves in defeat, for he has consumed us. As for infinite upon infinite, suppose he was right?

Let us pause. And pray.

Fairy Tale

The four sat at the supper table as usual, each gazing at the flickers of fire sashaying at the tips of the candles. The father would say grace any moment, but he seemed hesitant, distracted. All at once his head fell forward with such force that it split the walnut surface in two. The wife and two boys, too stunned to shriek, thought at first the father had played a joke on them. But no, the man was dead, his face contorted, swollen, his lips appallingly open and cracked. The wife and sons sat stiffly and watched as a brownish beetle crawled out of the father's mouth onto the table. Then, as truth anchored in, they screamed and rushed out of the room.

Years later the eldest son found himself holed up in a hovel, from where he rarely ventured. He saw spiders scurrying inside of his sole, foggy mirror. Insects shimmered across his flesh as he slept. He was kept alive through the good will and generosity of his fellow homeless. But he was no longer aware that he was alive. He sharpened his teeth on old rib-eye bones the dogs left behind.

The younger son had succeeded beyond anyone's wildest imaginings. He estimated his fortune in the billions. He produced low budget horror movies, invested in terrifying video games and toys. He forgot that he ever had an older brother or any other family. He told everyone that he had been orphaned at birth. He slept obliviously, never dreamed, believed in nothing. Once in a while he saw flickering at the corner of his eyes and assumed glaucoma. But he was too busy to see a doctor, all of whom he dismissed as frauds.

The mother, aging gracefully, still a looker, remarried, raised another child, a lissome, forlorn girl who rarely spoke. The new husband, a contractor, loved his wife. They lived in a splendid three-story brick house on an enviable avenue. Their lives were perfect, though the mother worried about three vertical ridges rising from her eyebrows to the hairline. No creams nor emollient softened or eradicated the ridges. She considered plastic surgery but resigned herself to the bleak fact that she was getting old and should ignore the ravages. Late one night, as she applied CeraVe to her cheek, she noticed a small, serrated tendril emerge from one of the ridges. Or thought she noticed anyway. She would get out the tweezers tomorrow. That's what you do with the past—you pluck it out.

Poetry Reading

Cat munches on a potato chip as she navigates the Subaru towards Blue Ridge College, I driving, she directing. The cartilage in my neck has stiffened in this sudden Arctic blast and I can no longer swivel it to check for maniacal drivers zooming out of merge lanes. That's her job now, assessing who's coming and going.

Dozens of police cars pass us, sirens screaming. A murderer is loose in the nearby mountains. A twenty-year-old military deserter who slaughtered his stepparents with an ax after years of abuse, even rape. Residents warned to lock down, schools closed. We worry about our daughters living in an apartment in Blue Ridge City, center of the action.

But the show must go on. Cat and I are en route to accompany the girls to a poetry reading sponsored by the College. A renowned poet paid fifty grand for a performance that will last half an hour.

We got off to a slow start, the postman late as usual. I didn't want to leave mail exposed in the box, especially the debit card scheduled to arrive. Thursday. We also want to minimize the traffic on Route 11. We avoid interstates obscenely bloated with eighteen-wheelers riding your bumpers,

Cat brings her knees up to rest on the dash above the glove compartment. "Wish they would catch that guy." I admire the shape of her thighs in black leggings.

I nod as still more squad cars whiz by. So much for avoiding traffic. We're late. The reading starts at seven and we still need to eat.

. . . .

Dulce greets us at the door. Her teacher, on lock down, cancelled class. Her sister, Trina, is still in class. The murderer has reportedly hidden in Parkway brush. He's said to be heavily armed and dangerous. So now it's waiting for Trina.

She rushes in breathlessly around five. "Sorry, he kept class overtime. What are we doing for eats?" This of course after hugs and greeting. We haven't seen our daughters in nearly a month.

We sit in conference at the dining table and plan out the night. Dulce suggests Popeye's, a bit out of the way but doable. I yearn for Popeye's red beans & rice, a smoky taste I have never forgotten

We misjudge the traffic again, I, driving hastily in mostly terra incognita, this time Dulce navigating since she has learned the geography of the area. Cat and Trina on the back seat whispering about something. Popeye's is so crowded that the line bends twice outside in the cold around the building. A spiffy new place, everybody after the new chicken sandwich voted best in America! We're worried about time—but too hungry not to eat. We decide on take-out so we can drive the food back to the College and eat in one of the Student Center cafeteria rooms if there's time. Otherwise, we will leave it in the car and reheat it later at the apartment. Trina is starving. So am I.

No red beans & rice or fried chicken for murderers hiding out in the wilderness.

. . . .

We manage to finish in the Student Center then trek to the Main Building where the reading will soon commence. The doors are locked. It's cold. A security guard finally opens up. A group of us hustle in and head towards the reading room, a beautiful place furnished with antiques, ottomans and Oriental rugs. The place fills quickly, mostly young people, artsy types, lots of ego and pretense. "I was reading Kierkegaard..." I overhear. And "Derrida" and "Lacan." A studious crowd. Some beautiful, stylish young women. One of the most tuition-expensive institutions in the country. Boasts its horses and stables. Could the murderer be out stalking the stables seeking a getaway horse? His vehicle has been found and impounded.

I choose a stuffed vintage armchair, Duce, Trina and Cat, the institutional chairs lined in rows. I'm surrounded by chatty, enthusiastic students and guests, three of them on the sofa behind my chair, one coughing violently. I shift my chair to the left. It's the moment before the famous poet, who sits up front beside his official escorts, one of whom will introduce him. I feel wedged in, bloated from Popeye's, out of sorts. I'm slightly envious of the besieged murderer camouflaged in underbrush, desperate, frantic.

The great poet rises to the podium. He recites short poems, one about pumping gas at a filling station, another, an anthill he accidentally demolished with his shoe, still another, his tenth birthday when he noticed only nine candles on the cake. And so on. About twenty- or thirty-minutes' worth for fifty grand.

Darkness envelopes us as we emerge from the Main Building, its porticos glistening with bluish fluorescent light. Light snow falls gently and silently. Reminds me of a painting by De Chirico. The moon has been full for two weeks. It's so cold I actually shiver as we make our way back to the Subaru parked across campus. It seems so long ago that Cat munched on the potato chip on our way here. I liked that moment, still like it. It seemed timeless and perfect.

Cat clutches the girls by their hands and tugs them along, ahead of me. She looks back and signals. "Hurry, Daddy-O, we're scared and cold." They swerve onto the grass because the sidewalk is blocked by a woman lying flat on her back and EMS people checking her out with blood pressure machines and syringes. Their halogen lights cast an eerie glow on the scene. I too swerve onto the grass but not before gazing into the prone woman's face, her eyes wide open. I'd seen her a while before at the reading. She had rushed out in medias res which, at the time, seemed rude. Had she been murdered? I did not want to know.

I plodded on trying to catch up with my family. Dulce looks back and smiles, waves. The snow has thickened, huge, wet discs now sticking to our caps and coats. It occurs to me that the murderer may have frozen to death in his cul de sac in these blue, blue mountains. Sirens still blare throughout the city. The Parkway has closed down. Apparently, more lock-down tomorrow for the area and environs. Indefinite lock-down.

. . . .

The road leading back to the apartment is narrow, dark and lonely. We drive by headlights and the light of the moon. We're almost out of fuel. The only gas station on this stretch is a vintage, no-brand dump only slightly refurbished since the 1970s. I pull up to the pumps, insert the credit card and smile to see ancient mechanical numbers clanking slowly along on the screen. Figure I may as well head for the bathroom while the deliquescent remains of dinosaurs fill the tank. Outside bathrooms! The station rises in front of a slope of bushes, trees and uncut grass. I'm thinking of the great poet's poem about pumping gas.

No sooner do I clutch the doorknob when it swings forcibly open, jerking me backwards. I now stand face to face with a crazed, dazed, desperate and haggard kid, his face pale as the moon. Our eyes lock and he oozes displeasure and anger. At first I thought stoned, drunk, a homeless wretch… but suddenly it dawns on me.

"You're the murderer," I gasp, realizing instantly that I'm at his mercy. Why did I say anything at all?

"Nah, you are," he laughs and scampers off into the woods, nearly slipping down the hillside. I hear the snapping of branches and commotion of something sliding down the hill.

"Good luck," I cry at the blackness surrounding us.

I don't bother to do my business inside the bathroom. I sort of zoom back to the Subaru to check on Cat and the girls. I slide breathlessly behind the wheel.

"You ok, Daddy? You look frazzled," Dulce's voice from the back seat. Now they're all staring at me. "Something happened over there?" Cat asks. She has propped her knees against the dash again. Those wonderful leggings.

"Just tired from all the driving and rushing about. I'm ok. Let's just go home and take it easy for a while."

Trina wants to know what I thought about the poetry reading. Many of her classmates and professors attended. She was assigned to write a response.

Frenzied sirens recede from us in another direction. "Sounds like they found him! Cat exclaims.

"Could be," I grunt, and "Best poetry reading ever, Trina." I buckle up, slip into drive and step on the gas.

Degas and the Turkey Buzzard

An ill-spirited, preoccupied Edgar Degas stood on the wharf, canvass suitcases dangling from each hand. He felt weak, almost faint and dreary. He feared he was going blind and had crossed the Atlantic in 1872 to rest his eyes in the lazy, Mesozoic jungle he expected New Orleans to be, an outpost where his mother's side of the family happened to reside. Family members promised to meet him at the river, but so far no one had shown up. An old, stooped porter appeared at his side. "Take yo' bags, mistah? Costes a quawta." Degas apprized the man. Eighty years old if a day and still toting luggage for quarters. He felt touched, anchored in grief, for the man, for the world, for himself.

"Sir," he said, "I am touched by your offer, but I think it best if I carry my own bags. One of them contains my art equipment, and I can't take any chances."

The porter scratched his wooly, gray hair and grinned. "I knew you was a awtist. You got dat look. Like Mistah Awdabun, when he was chere befo da Civil Waw."

Degas didn't hear a word of it. His attention had shifted abruptly to two wooden pilings rising from the wharf. On one of them squatted a Louisiana Brown Pelican, which he recognized from picture books, but something he could scarcely imagine perched on the other, the ugliest, most forlorn and mean-looking creature he had ever seen. A bird, no doubt, but pre-historic, spawned in hell. Its head amounted to an ill-shaped, extravagant reddish beak attached to a kind of pole-like, scaly neck that could recede into or extend from its gawky body. Degas and the bird eyed each other with suspicion.

"What, my friend, is that horrible animal?" he asked the porter.

The porter swiveled his head toward the direction Degas pointed, then laughed a long, deep, effluvial guffaw. "Dat be a toikey buzzid. Mistah Awdabun drew him too. You gonna draw him? Looks like sin. But lemme tell you, dat boid is clean. Don't kill nothin' neitha. Eats lots of ve-ge-tebles cause dat beak is weak. It feasts on dead animals only if dey awready town up by dogs. Dey live in families, like us, and take baths all da live long day. Just got a bum rap because dey so ugly. Dem nice boids. Don't go nearby cause it shoot vomit on you, its only weapon."

"Turkey buzzard," Degas repeated as if entranced, "turkey buzzard."

Half an hour later, when his family arrived to bring him home, he still stood fixed in the same spot, gazing at the bird.

As if in a stupor he repeated the words "turkey buzzard" during the entire carriage ride to Esplanade Avenue. The family looked at each other with raised eyebrows and tapped their temples. After all, what did they know about this distant cousin and brother beyond that he painted pictures of Parisian chorus girls and ballet dancers?

Degas rarely left the house on Esplanade. His eyes ached. He had come to New Orleans to rest and visit the "Creole" branch of his family, but his vision of the turkey buzzard continued to haunt him. An ominous gargoyle he couldn't drive out of his mind. For weeks varied relatives found him pacing his quarters muttering "turkey buzzard." *Clean. Live in families. And yet... feasting on the dead. Like us.*

His mother's side of the clan had lost a fortune during Reconstruction but at the same time managed to retain status and a solid circuit of social connections. One of the heroes of the American Civil War, General Beauregard, had actually sought him out in Paris and commissioned him to execute a portrait of his nieces. Degas complied but had to endure disheveled, haggard Beauregard's constant weeping over a lost love, Marie Laveau, the legendary voo doo queen. Or perhaps Marie's daughter or granddaughter, since Marie the First had died in 1835. Nor was the exotic copper coloring of the nieces and their sultry almost oriental eyes lost on the painter, although none of these features would show up in the portrait.

But he hardly had time to ponder the implications, what with the mad rush or family obligations and work. His older brother Achille had sailed to France and would soon shoot the husband of his mistress on the steps of the Paris Bourse. The younger brother Rene had married cousin Estelle, who *was* blind! What Degas feared! During his sojourn to New Orleans Estelle intrigued Degas and became his favorite model. His portraits of her, standing by a window perhaps or performing some domestic duty requiring neither sight nor mind, revealed superficial decorum, a satiation of domestic fullness, even as they seethed with forbidding dark shadows and ponderous melancholy. Nor could his work distract him from the memory of his mother's toilsome depression. Always worry over something. He should never have left Paris. And now he was in love with his brother's wife!

Or did her plight merely fascinate him? He found her irrelevant, her limited mobility, her narrow world, her aristocratic pretense and whiny demands. Since when could the blind demand anything at all? His eyes felt more strained than ever. Estelle suggested he wash them with a diluted dose of Dr. Tichenor's Antiseptic. "Only half a drop in a quart of water," she warned. "Otherwise, you'll wish you were blind."

"Dr. Tichenor's?"

"Yes, a friend of the family. He comes round every so often to inform us about some grand scheme he has to transform the city into a feudal aristocracy through mass merchandising. I thought that had already come to pass. I hear they're drinking his antiseptic on Bourbon Street in preference to absinthe and anisette."

"I must try it, "Degas mused as a turkey buzzard crashed through one of the parlor windows.

"Horrid, vile animals!" cried Estelle. "Somebody is going to die."

Degas rushed from the room, panting, awash in sweat. It was dusk and he felt his eyes could tolerate the gentle glow of the oil lamps that lined Esplanade Avenue. He trotted down the steps of the cottage, crossed the street and walked swiftly on the neutral ground toward the river. Absorbed in thought, he found himself suddenly frozen in place, frozen, as if the particular ground on which he now stood had lured him forth. He watched the city disintegrate before his eyes, retrogress into the primeval bogs and miasma out of which it once arose. He stood beside a shadowy figure of the once on-and-off Governor of Louisiana, Jean Baptiste LeMoyne, Sieur de Bienville, commissioned in 1718 by the French sovereign to build a city near the mouth of the Mississippi.

Bienville stood knee deep in a hazy cypress swamp thick with alligators and mosquitoes swollen as figs, gazing into what seemed empty space—to the dismay of his fidgety and impatient companions. His eyes glowed softly like hematite. He waved a finger and signaled. "This is it," he said loud enough for all in the group to hear, "this is the spot." Renegade Natchez and Chickasaw might attack any moment. Bienville's companions glanced nervously at each other. He would leave them, a band of fifty or so grizzled salt smugglers, to clear the swamp and erect the first shacks that would commemorate the founding of

New Orleans.

Bienville had been here before, in 1699, and knew even then, despite political friction from every quarter, that this patch of swamp nestled within the river's spectacular crescent was both practical and magical. He had lived a rugged, frontier life all of his thirty-seven years; despite his blood of minor nobility, he had no friends at court. hey were plotting against him, had tried to replace him on numerous occasions. But the replacements always died en route across the sea! The present undertaking was preposterous. Alligators, lagoons and savages! But then, the Age of Reason had not yet flattened the world. Montesquieu, Diderot, D'Alembert and Voltaire would create their stir at mid-century. So there was still time. Anything was possible. No one had yet stormed the Bastille or beheaded the king.

Degas stared at a dilapidated but still grand three-story mansion with boarded windows and rotten front steps. Three tiers of Victorian balustrades had collapsed and lay in heaps on the balconies. Stagnant New Orleans humidity had dissolved the paint on the now gray, soggy and mournful weather boards. A sign hung below the rusted mailbox: FOR RENT. Bienville's eyes had focused upon the remains of a venerable, gnarled cypress, slick with lichen, its crevices and knotholes teeming with black snakes, bloated grackles and turkey buzzards cawing from sloped branches. For a moment Degas saw the cypress as well, the mansion had vanished, but he shook his head like a dog shedding water and blinked rapidly to steady his sight. He thought something might be wrong with him, for as of late he was seeing things, not hallucinations exactly, but fleeting, shadowy images at the fringes of his eyes—trees, animals, primitive human figures. Just tired, he assured himself, never enough sleep. Time to drag himself back to the house, work, ignore his relatives ranting about carpetbaggers.

He took the return walk slowly, with determined serenity, on the banquet this time. The vision of New Orleans as a primitive, prehistoric wilderness had drained him. The Gallic veneer, the pretense, the nerve! The place was a joke, not like Paris at all, not civilized, despite his memories of his mother protesting just the opposite. She had languished overseas, missed the balls and fetes and gaiety of her Creole set. As if there weren't enough to see and do in Paris! As he walked he marveled at the seemingly endless rows of grandiose mansions along the avenue. Where had all the money come from? Who lived in them?

At the intersection of Rampart Street and Esplanade he nearly tripped over a hunched human form squatting on the corner. "Merde!" he cried, stumbling for balance, "What in the hell are you doing? I could have broken my neck!"

The form slowly lifted its head, a head draped with burlap hood. Human all right, but as Degas now saw, shrouded entirely in sackcloth. Ashes smudged into the forehead.

"I am a penitent," the man sighed. "I have been to your Mardi Gras."

"Not *my* Mardi Gras, sir, I am merely a visitor to this impossible city."

"As am I. Duke Alexis Alexandrovitch Romanoff at your disposal, or service, or whatever the case, preparing to dispatch for terra incognita. Do not, I beseech you, fall in love with American women. Behold your fate in the mirror of me, fallen from eminence to disgrace and disfigurement. A woman does not cast a glance upon a broken tree. Fine line, eh? Someone will take credit for it in the future, I guarantee."

"What?"

"Lydia!" the man wailed.

Degas took no pity on the obviously crestfallen, wretched specimen. "Why loiter in this desolate neighborhood? Why squat like a beast? Go to Paris, pay for a chorus girl."

"I thus make my obeisance to the city that humbled me in Lentan posture and guise. I have absconded from my vessel and bodyguards. But just for an hour or so. Then it's adieu for me, forever. Thank you, kind friend, for the sparse conversation, for making bodily contact with me, however fortuitous and brutal. I can leave now in peace. I believe I may drown at sea. Make sure you try the local ravioli."

Degas shook his head, spat and trudged onward toward Bayou Road. "Imposter," he growled under his breath. "Duke, ha! Romanoff! Get back to your precious Easter eggs and filigree. Why must the tramps of this city concoct illusions of noble lineage? Mardi Gras, I was there too. Once is enough. Rabble groveling for trinkets. I prefer the cemeteries. I *must* get back to France."

Crème de Menth

After every holiday meal we would all drink creme de menthe from long-stemmed crystal glasses that had belonged to my great-great-grandmother. Life seemed slower, more elegant in those days, and we took hand-stitched lace tablecloths, linen napkins with sterling rings and Bavarian china as quite natural frills to our never less than sumptuous feasts. Creme de menthe, which looks like liquid emerald, fit in perfectly. The only problem was that we all hated it.

Its minty vapors burned my eyes, and its texture was a thick, sugary syrup that we could hardly swallow without gagging. But never once did I dream of simply refusing to hold out the glass when my grandfather, who presided over the gatherings with the aplomb of a Roman emperor, poured the inch or so allotted to us kids.

I made my move when I was eighteen. My father had assumed the duties of pouring, but for some reason he lacked the clout of my grandfather; perhaps he had come to grasp the absurdity of such forced rituals. He motioned for me to pass my glass, and I hesitated, then said, "No, I don't like it much." My father looked astonished, sad, crushed, yet he seemed to have expected such a turn, even to understand. He shrugged and poured for my sister, who longed to refuse as well. But we'd have to wait another year or so for her courage to blossom.

Thereafter the creme de menthe appeared every holiday as usual, but the only drinkers were my grandparents, mother and father. They didn't push it on my sister or me or our spouses. I gloated over having helped defeat a useless and distasteful vestige and pretended not to notice the sickening green soup that clung to the crystal glasses like algae.

On Christmas day, years later, I find myself in a house full of new people—new wives, strange children, replacement brothers- and sisters-in-law. The only ones left from the old days are my mother and sister. After lunch I realize she has not broken out the creme de menthe. She sits distant and feeble at the head of the table.

I go over to a cabinet where I know I'll find both the long-stemmed glasses and a dusty green bottle. I arrange all on a tray and return, look

Louis Gallo

my smiling mother in the eye.

"It's time," I announce, passing the glasses around. My sister, who has not touched creme de menthe in years, is surprised but eager. And we all drink smoothly, everyone, except me that is, gagging as usual. But like my grandfather and father, I am determined to drain my glass.

I single out the most introspective grandchild, the one most like me, the one who already grieves over the past. "Come here, boy," I say, and he comes, excited because he loves but is also afraid of me. We have rarely talked although I have had my eye on him.

"How do you like creme de menthe?" I ask.

"Yuk!" he says.

"That's true," I say, "but some things you just have to do."

He shakes his head.

I pour a tiny bit more into my glass, drink and pass it to him. "One day these glasses will be yours. You know what that means?"

"Yes," he whispers sadly, before running off to play, as if it were a dark secret too terrible to bear.

The Player

This used to be a fun house/
But now it's full of evil clowns...
    —Pink

I drift into the shady joint, nothing else to do, and watch a few sharks perform their torque on green felt. Not my game though. I'm partial to pin balls, the older and more wooden, the better. Most are dormant, asleep, ignored by the young punks who opt for ivory or electronic games of mayhem and massacre. Yet two quarters will catapult these relics into frenzy after all these years and sweaty palms. Little swatches of Las Vegas right here in Nowhere.

Lisa, stalked by identical twins who scream, hiss, and brandish garden clippers, swallows ten mg. of Ativan each day. Uncle George molested his niece Casey when on her fourth birthday he set her on his lap. The god Pan makes love to Rhonda, Rachel and Ashley, who turn to lithium, Wellbutrin, Prozac, and kill sex with chemicals. Vanessa smells dead babies in the earth. Kathleen watches blood trickle from her nostrils, eye sockets and ears. Kelly describes her night sweats and tremors as just punishments for a wicked life. Luci has befriended Christ and can talk of nothing else. Christ is an ice cube in her non-caloric sweetened tea. Suzy has lost twenty pounds. Her teeth spin like the blades of a propeller. Stephanie has been exorcized by a voo doo priest in New Orleans.

These reports, some whispered in the dark, some broadcast over PA systems at rallies, have little effect on our lives. We weep perhaps and stagger through each new day like drunks. We have problems of our own. We have inherited the women, our mothers, daughters and lovers, and yearn to seal them in capsules which not even a single microbe much less bands of despoilers can puncture. Yet safety too is abusive and cruel. So we shrug and bear impotent witness as the ball rambles where it may. We flip madly, curse, pound the worn sides of the machine, until, inevitably, it slips through, thuds into a hole. The lights and buzzers screech TILT. We drift away, nod to a rare next player who drops silver into the hungry slits. Outside, in the glare of this lean street, Eve leans against a light pole. She is scandalously clad and stricken with flesh. We want her and we don't want her.

Never Start or End a Story with a Dream

Yeah, a dream all right, or was, few nights ago, the best dream of my life because when so cocooned I felt the serenity of timelessness, love, beauty, all that and more... so let me record it now before, as all dreams, it dissolves:

I step into a New Orleans café full of art deco prints on the walls. It resembles the old Marti's Restaurant on Rampart except Marti's has shifted on its axis and is now horizontal to Canal Street up yonder... and everything behind Marti's is chaos, evil, scary, dark, whereas all affronting it–light and bustle, the usual Quarter...

Well, I step in and scout for a booth and find one in the middle of the aisle, so I slide over to the window draped with bamboo shades, and soon a middle-aged waitress appears, her wrinkles and eroded face alarming, and I tell her I'm waiting for someone and can't order yet. She huffs away as you approach from behind and slide softly beside me and I'm overjoyed to see you and smile a big one and you lean against my shoulder, and we hook into each other's eyes and can't stop smiling...

"Hey You," I grin, and you reply, "Hey you," and grin, and we're smiling like idiots, lips stretched to our temples in gladness, and I say again, "Hey you," and you, "Hey you," and we're pressed together, you in a green floral shirt and those wondrous tight jeans I love and afflicts all other girls with pangs of jealousy. I wrap my arm around you, and grin again "Hey you," and we sort of forget we were to meet and head out for the airport for a flight to Manhattan.

We just linger, embracing, and I smell the essence of you, the scent of ambrosia, of youth, and I inhale you, inhale and reel with delight and thanksgiving, for in this dream I am about twenty-eight, and you, twenty-two, and we're young and unencumbered and mad over each other, and nothing else matters, the way I like it, nothing to matter, and time obliterates itself, and I lick your cheek and taste you, and feel the warmth of your arms and shoulders and there is nothing, no

Louis Gallo

amount of money, no act of Congress to save the planet, no cure for cancer, there is nothing I would trade for this moment for, a moment the dream magic makes eternal, and "Hey You," I laugh again, and you, "Hey You too"...

And then it ended, how a door slams shut, and I lay flat on the bed, my face smashed into the mattress, feeing horrible and desolate–and understood that real doors can never be reopened.

Chamber Music

On Saturday evenings Liberato's house blazed with light that poured like molten butter from cracks in every window shutter. As the cousins rallied in their front yards or in the street and women swayed on front porch swings and gossiped, as locusts buzzed in every tree in the city, a sweet melodic perfume would seep out of his uncle's house to intoxicate the neighborhood. Paw, Achille, Liberato and one or two other musicians would get together for a few hours to play a strict repertoire of chamber music by Mozart, Beethoven, Schubert, Brahms and Dvorak. Paw played violin and viola, Achille played flute and Liberato strained at the cello (Paw always said Liberato couldn't play worth a damn), and they sounded magical to Jake, who in pursuit of one cousin or another would often pause in the alley beneath Liberato's parlor window to listen. It would be many years before he could name the piece as such, but in fact he first heard Schubert's celestial "Quintet in C" as he stood almost paralyzed in that dark gloomy alley with Dougie, who could not hear the music and badgered Jake to get on with whatever game they were playing. Achille told his son years later that when they played Schubert, they all cried; sometimes their tears splattered onto the scores and smudged out the notes altogether. Nina, not Italian but Austrian, played with the group for a short while and chided the grown men for their girlish sentimentality.

"Schubert was German," Paw cried, "and he wrote the stuff!"

"He wrote it to defeat Italians," Nina smirked, "which is not difficult."

This was also the time of Vadish, the mad Lithuanian pianist who sometimes showed up to play with the group. Liberato allowed him to touch only the keyboard of a beat-up old Steinway because he distrusted Slavic fingertips. "They're probably corrosive," he told his brother. So Vadish banged on a piano that no one could ever tune. The instrument required major carpentry work whenever Vadish finished with it, for he did indeed destroy whatever he touched.

Vadish howled obscenities when he played. He couldn't help himself. His passion knew no limits. They all thought he would have a stroke because the veins in his temples bulged and pulsated in tempo with the music.

Vadish had a strange life, to say the least. His father did business in Turkey when Vadish was only a lad. One day he forgot his son on a curb outside a warehouse where he heatedly negotiated over some crates of Sobranie. At that time certain priests paid brigands a small fortune for delivery of young boys to a secret chapel. The priests, obsessed with the reputation of their a capella choir, routinely castrated the boys—and I mean they sliced everything—hoping to cultivate a truly angelic voice that would make their music renowned worldwide. So Vadish became a nine-year-old eunuch in a Turkish choir. They say his father never missed him, forgot in fact that he had a son.

It turned out Vadish couldn't sing—they said he sounded like a hive of bees trapped under a washtub—so the priests dumped him into the most disreputable neighborhood in all Istanbul, where they disposed of the flops. Pirates prowled this neighborhood in search of children they could sell into white slavery, and they soon pounced on Vadish, stuffed him into a burlap sack and dropped him into a crate full of cargo. He wound up in Cairo working for an Egyptian shipping magnate who fancied himself the latest incarnation of Ramses II. The master was not harsh or abusive, however, and Vadish forfeited several opportunities to escape. His master trusted Vadish to wash and perfume his favorite concubines with spices and unguents since the boy was a eunuch, though he could not have guessed that as Vadish reached puberty, his member started to re-grow, like a chameleon's tail. By fourteen, Vadish could boast full restoration—to the delight of his master's harem. But he grew weary of the boredom of servitude and the concubines' salacious entreaties.

One day, while prowling the master's library, he came across a primer for piano. He felt transported and scrutinized the keyboard illustrations, the staves and depictions of notes, the key signatures and prompts. A desire to play seized him, but the master had a tin ear and possessed no musical instruments. So Vadish taped together several sheets of paper, reproduced a keyboard to scale with ink pens and practiced arpeggios on this drawing for months. He spent every spare moment playing this paper keyboard, which is how he mastered the piano. His urge to touch a real piano became so orgasmic that he abandoned the master and sought his fortune in the streets of Cairo.

One day he wandered into a joint that catered to American sailors and spotted a honky-tonk upright in the corner. He wiped spider webs from the keys and started to play. People outside heard his phenomenal music and rushed into the bar and pretty soon the place was packed. The owner offered Vadish a job on the spot. He remained with the bar until a maestro from some minor American symphony touring Cairo happened to stop in for a drink. When he heard Vadish he advanced toward the piano, gazed into the boy's eyes and said, "If you don't come to America with me, I will shoot you on the spot." He patted his corduroy jacket as if to suggest he carried a weapon in the inner pocket. "I'll make you a star," he went on. "You'll be in Carnegie Hall before the year's over."

The rest is history. Vadish did acquire a stellar reputation in America for a while, but he was volatile and unstable and could not stop shrieking obscenities when he played. Once, during a performance of a Rachmaninoff's Third Piano Concerto, he howled, "It's so fucking beautiful! Listen you, assholes, this is what beauty sounds like!" The entire audience fled the performance hall in protest. He attempted control by hurling himself violently against the nearest wall, like a truck rushing up the runaway ramp. But in the end nothing worked. Vadish finally destroyed his career in classical music altogether and had to take whatever jobs he could find. Any piano at all lured him to it as if by magnetic force, and he found himself reduced to a row of Greek bars on Decatur Street, where the regulars regarded obscenities as normal. He had stowed to New Orleans on a banana boat because someone told him that you didn't need money to live the good life in such a phantasmal city. He even played in the symphony upon his arrival, before its conductor realized his affliction was chronic.

Here he met Nina, who found him attractive, though who knows why? Who can account for the tastes of women, my boy? I saw Vadish a few times. His willowy hair flew out in every direction and floated above his head as if detached. He was ghastly pale, almost translucent. He reminded me of one of those albino night lizards whose inner organs are visible through their skin. He wore a royal purple cape eaten ragged by moths and a pair of American cowboy boots. He had a certain nobility though, like a disreputable aristocrat gone to seed. A kind of ragged Chopin, whom George Sand called affectionately 'My little corpse.' They say that at the end gnats constantly swarmed Vadish's head like pathetic little Furies. He cared for nothing at all but music. Music, he said, "is my food." No one knew where he lived or

Louis Gallo

how he survived. He simply showed up at your uncle's house from time to time, usually breathless and by that time raving drunk, swatting at the gnats with his lanky spaghetti-like fingers.

We heard later that he had some sort of seizure on Canal Street, where he had taken to begging with a tin cup. He knew something was wrong when the gnats abandoned him in a frenzied diaspora. Witnesses say he literally exploded. Parts of his body flew out in every direction. A blind man begging with him said his last words were "Holy shit, I'm fucking shrapnel!"

Maryjane

'd always resisted because the thought of losing reason, of irrational mayhem, terrified me more than disease or nuclear annihilation. But by twenty-two the mind per se no longer thrilled; I'd studied Plato, Kant, even that monster Hegel–and seemed no better off. Not that I wasn't curious or aching to be cool. Long hair, beard, wire-rim glasses, I had them, so all I lacked was the temptation, which soon came in the form of two girls who invited me out to a farmhouse in Nebraska, just the three of us in a cabin beside a field bloated with cows, a mile or so into the fecund heartland.

Soon enough they break out the joints, toke and pass one to me. Not cool, but I resist, tell them that I'd tried before (a lie) and the fumes have no effect. Then the blond leans over on the sofa where we had squeezed together and kisses me. "For me?" she asks with the sweetness of honeysuckle and jasmine. Ok, ok, I say, but just a little, and mimicking her, suck in a lungful, hold it steady, then exhale in a gush. I do this maybe four times; it isn't much. Fifteen minutes later I shake my head, see, nothing… I must be immune.

The brunette asks me to fetch a bag of pretzels from the table and some orange juice in the fridge. No big deal, sure, but really, I say, I don't feel a thing. Then I stand up. The world swirls beneath my feet as I grope for the pretzels. I lose all sense of direction and offer them a hall tree. The girls giggle in another dimension. Where are we? Who are we? What time is it? The vestiges of thought explode like confetti. I feel vaguely nauseous but don't care because the new feeling, like a first orgasm, is better. Vertigo doesn't count, the noble mind is a fraud, that joyous confusion, beautiful and hungry… recalling, with once again the agency of reason, I can't say whether I passed out or not, if we all had sex or not, how long I laughed stupidly, whether I threw up or peed on one of the cows… though I remember the girls, Lenore and Ulalume, and send them a belated *thanks*.

We've lost touch though I'm tempted to sleuth their whereabouts. And, alas, I no longer touch the stuff, though it has nothing to do with the paltry triumph of reason or moral reform. Just makes me cold and jittery, horrified, and like some shaman of old I've seen my bones shattered on inevitable crags, I've seen enemies oozing out of the plumbing, I've heard the wails and shrieks of demons. And I forgot to say that when I left that cabin, I wound up driving my Fiat Spider not on the interstate but across some meadow toward a pond and had no idea where I was or how I got there or what would happen next or if anything ever happens next.

Monstrosity

I passed a flatbed truck on I-81 a few hours ago, a truck that bore on its flatness this monstrous piece of, I assume, equipment. The thing was massive and rusted and flared out in all directions with endless sprockets and gears and springs, levers, turbines, bolts.

I wondered about its possible use, no doubt industrial, maybe military... it almost resembled the skeleton of some ancient alien beast, the sort of thing space travelers encounter in the movies when they explore some erratic blips on their oscilloscopes.

If women ruled the world, I thought, no such behemoth would have been constructed; or if we had remained proto-human, the thing, sunken in some bog, might be worshipped. I glance over at the driver of the truck as I passed. He wore a baseball cap and a cigar butt dangled from his lip as he thumped the dash with his free palm to some music I could not hear. Why do I presume country?

He seemed an ordinary enough fellow hauling a cargo of pure evil to a hive of clandestine saboteurs—merely the delivery boy who, if questioned, might snap *I don't know nothing.*

And at this moment I spin backwards in time to a cave in Cumae where the sibyl, enshrouded in incense and smoke, intones gibberish we once took as wisdom.

We dismiss such muttering as superstition, magic, primitive, worthless babble; we deem the monstrosity as progress. We flick on the lights and our houses glow.

Miss Swander

Piano lessons seemed a breeze next to kindergarten. Jake had clung to Violet's hand and squirmed fiercely the entire six blocks to McDonogh 9 as she escorted him to school and up the stairs into the cheerful classroom of Miss Swander, his first schoolteacher, a small, stooped and wiry woman with hair the texture of pine needles. The teacher gushed with enthusiasm as she welcomed Violet into the room. Violet told him later that Miss Swander had caught smallpox as a child, which accounted for the craters on her face as well as the curvature of her spine. One night when she was only seven years old Miss Swander woke to a chilling sweat and dread in her heart. She opened her eyes to see the smallpox demon zigzag above her face, buzzing like a horse fly. She rolled over on her stomach and pulled the pillow over her head, but the demon dove into the back of her neck, gnawed at her flesh and burrowed in, spreading pathogens into her bones and blood. Her fever raged for days until Father Rinaldi of St. Rosa de Lima administered extreme unction. Miss Swander's distraught father prayed to St. Rosa and begged for his child's life. He promised to repair the stained glass of the church windows for the rest of his days if she granted his wish.

Within two hours Miss Swander's fever abated, she opened her eyes for the first time since she saw the demon and meekly asked for a slice of king cake. The next day she hopped out of bed and, except for her disfigurement, proved the healthiest child in the neighborhood. Her strength became extraordinary. Still only seven, the child could lift her father's Packard by the chrome bumper and hold it steadily two feet off the ground. She could thrash any boy in her neighborhood, even many grown men, though she only fought in self-defense. There was not a malicious corpuscle in her body.

One morning when she was away at school Mr. Swander ransacked his daughter's room in search of the smallpox demon. He found an evil red insect with tiny horns protruding from its head; he tempted it into a mayonnaise jar with a chunk of rotten crawfish and drowned it in his own urine. The insect turned black, sizzled, clawed frantically at the sides of the glass and then, to Mr. Swander's amazement, exploded into hundreds of small nuggets that resembled tiny four o'clock seeds. He drained the urine, poured the seeds into a lead box and soldered it shut, then buried it six feet below ground. He thanked St.Rosa and spent every spare minute of the rest of his life repairing the church's windows, for as soon as he replaced glass or resoldered one, another would break in relentless, merciless succession. At age ninety he perished of chronic lead poisoning. His doctors marveled over the man's constitution; the amount of lead in his body would have killed a battalion of soldiers. When Miss Swander bent over to kiss her father's corpse goodbye, she tasted metal, a taste she could never brush or gargle away. Some said it accounted for the silverish tint to her lips.

"And how's the young man today?" Miss Swander squinted down at Jake over her prince-nez.

"Well…" Violet raised her eyebrows.

"Oh, pooh," Miss Swander said, cupping his head with her palm, "we'll just have to stop that whimpering, won't we?"

Jake despised the woman instantly. It was one thing to whimper but quite another to be exposed in front of all the other children by someone who had probably never whimpered in her life, who could not possibly grasp the urgent need to whimper.

He preferred to keep his Kindergarten reputation a secret, for he was quite aware that he had lost control. He spent an entire week self-exiled in the sandbox of Miss Swander's merry class, refusing to participate or turn the pages of his workbook or even sit next to the other students at their little lacquered tables, detesting his so-called locker, which smelled like vomit. His grief knew no limit; his heart was broken; his mother had abandoned him. Never did he blame or hold it against her; Violet would not desert him unless forced into it. Thus silently and with mounting displeasure he unleashed his torrential woe upon Miss Swander.

The teacher finally capitulated and allowed him to sulk and grieve, the way he chose to spend his entire day. During recess he sought out sacred spots on the school grounds beside the azalea bushes or near the row of startling poinsettias whose lush red blossoms looked edible, places where his mother had walked with him or hugged him goodbye; or he hovered with longing near the unscalable wire fence that separated him from her and everything he knew, as a prisoner clings to the very bars which make freedom a dream. The places his mother had traversed were magical, spiritual sites, and he reasoned that if he returned to them, rooted himself in place for hour on end, he might reverse history, bring her back, end the dismay which swept him away from not only her and Columbus Street but even himself.

Yet as time passed he drifted away from the magic places, for obviously their magic did not work, his mother did not solidify in thin air, he was not instantly transported back to Columbus Street. One day he crept out of the sandbox toward Miss Swander's desk and whispered into her ear that he wanted now to assume his place at one of the tables. He plunged himself into the baleful workshop exercises with the solemnity of a scholar, took his locker in stride, joshed around with the children in his class, who weren't so bad after all, and in effect became a model student. It had become clear that no one would tolerate any less, that he would otherwise have soon become one of the very neighborhood coo-coos he and everybody else made fun of and taunted.

And he succeeded in making his first real friend outside the family, that skinny boy Dave Silner who taught him all the dirty words and just so happened to live on the next block of Columbus Street. It was Dave who introduced Jake to such unspeakable secrets that he reeled simultaneously with horror and unquenchable curiosity. Dave had a deck of playing cards that depicted a fat young woman with skin pale as tissue engaged in fellatio with a naked man whose body was so hairy Jake could not tell if he were man or beast. The first time Jake saw the card he felt his heart catapult. The sight destroyed his peace of mind for weeks. He could think of nothing else, though he didn't know what the act meant or why the naked people would resort to such ignominy. Yet they looked exceedingly happy. The playing card implied scandalous, mysterious vices–and incontestable pleasures–lying dimly ahead in the future, a future he longed to leap into, a future he prayed kept its distance.

St. Jude

'd spent yesterday afternoon examining the floor-to-ceiling golden and silver replicas of moribund human organs on display at St. Jude's International Shrine of the Hopeless, about a fifteen-minute trek from my apartment. Thousands of tiny organs, people who were diseased, people who were cured, those praying to be cured, those lighting votive candles on the altar and dropping coins and cash into the collection boxes, people rubbing rosary beads as they hunched in some rear pew, people at wit's end because illness had sabotaged their lives, had constricted their futures, had eaten them alive. I told Genevieve that I wanted to write a story on this place for the local rag, *En Courant*, where I worked as free-lance. But the real reason I went was that, as usual, I thought I was dying. I say as usual because I've thought about dying every moment of my life, from the dim reptilian memories of my early childhood to the present moment.

At one point I was convinced I would die at seven years old because of some strange spongy little lump that had formed on my right earlobe. I guess I was six then, maybe five. I walked about moping, pinching the lobe at all times between fingers to make sure the lump hadn't grown or warped or multiplied. My grandmother kneaded some Dr. Tichenor's into the lump—she said Dr. Tichenor's cured everything. Sure enough, the lump dissolved in a few days. What am I dying of now? Of everything. I have every disease known to man and some new ones not yet discovered. What are my symptoms? Pretty vague here, feeling fuzzy and disoriented and riddled with malaise, maybe faint though I've never fainted, tweaks of pain in one part of the body or the other, vague amorphous symptoms accompanied by a sense of dread and defeat.

The little tacked-on organs made it worse so I rushed out of the place onto Rampart and nearly got hit by a tourist buggy full of Iowans clutching Hurricane drinks. A few yards up the buggy donkey dropped dead of a heat stroke and two-seats worth of tourists were flung asunder. A middle-aged man wearing an Old Fart t-shirt landed in a fresh pile of dung deposited by the defunct donkey upon its demise.

Louis Gallo

That donkey was too horrific to think about.

Gender Hijinks

He told her she was beautiful, but she scoffed, my lower lip sticks out too far.

He said that's what he loved about her lower lip. My knees are bony, she said, lifting her skirt.

See? Ugly. No, he said, perfect knees. My eyes are like saucers, she whined, but he—big eyes, a classic sign of beauty, and green too, the rarest color. My breasts are too small, she groaned, whereupon he—just right, not udders, not acorns, just so right. And my ass, she sighed, it has ripples, it sags.

But he, no ripples, no sags, your ass is a glorious work of art. Would you prefer that I say it resembles a soft boulder?

Such a pig, she growled, is that all you think about? Men! You're obsessed with how we look. What about me? What about my soul, my mind, my feelings and my personality?

Yeah, he nodded, you could work on that last one.

See! See! What did I tell you! I think you'd better leave now.

And he—but I love you.

Wittgenstein: A Micro-Biography

The young man detested their silly giggling in the cafes. Bright ribbons fluttered in the usual girls' hair. Psychoanalysts passed in silken, black carriages. Assassination and hemophilia troubled the empire. A new theory of light drove him into cold, dim rooms. He stood on a corner in Vienna and felt inches shorter. A horse snorted. The new century severed time like an ax. "Reality begets language!" he cried to a startled passerby.

That same reality betrayed him. He never smiled, stroked a severe violin as his brothers killed themselves. His youthful decorum hardened into zeal and he listened for breathing beneath the ink. He imagined words so refined they split throats even as safer, more prudent words floated through his mind like balloons. He was wrong. There was only language. He stopped talking and disappeared for years.

We find him next sulking on the patios of wry philologists. The infinite but unbounded universe had expanded. War hero, school master, common gardener, he entertained the philological wives: "Philosophy," he teased, "is a battle against the bewitchment of an intelligence by means of language." He accompanied students to Walt Disney movies in a personal dome of gloom, insisting his aim was "to show the fly the way out of the fly bottle."

On the day he died he shot up in bed, wild-eyed, beseeched his last disciple, "Tell them I've lived a wonderful life!"

Plutonium

'm leaning against the alligatored weather boards of the PE building behind the school. Not a building really, just a kind of make-shift shack where we huddle when it rains. It's the ten-minute break between classes and I'm thinking about something we just learned in science the period before: missiles in Cuba aimed straight for us.

The science teacher tries to scare us. He admits it during class. "The best way to learn something is when it frightens you. Then you don't forget." So today he talked about atomic bombs and plutonium. "One speck of it in the atmosphere," he said, "will kill one hundred thousand people."

So this is what's on my mind, not the hundreds of kids kicking balls in the dusty field or hanging out on the concrete steps waiting for the cafeteria to open, or the ones just loitering over by the fence trying to sneak in a smoke. I don't even notice that the meanest, biggest, toughest punk in school is headed my way. Sonny Busso. He's flunked a few times and looks like a man, not one of us kids. I heard he shaves three times a day. He's probably twenty years old to look at him.

Suddenly he's standing, no swaying, right in front of me and then I do notice. I've got to look up to catch his gaze. "Hey, kid," he says, "gimme a quarter."

I stuff my hands tightly into my khaki pockets. "I don't have a quarter," I say. I do in fact have a quarter and it's clutched in my left fist, but I have resolved never to give Sonny Busso another.

Sonny gazes at me, almost stunned it seems. Everybody gives him quarters every day. He's a rich man. Then he slaps me across the face, just like that, whack… and I don't see stars, as they say you do, but cans of Breast-o-Chicken tuna, opened cans with juice dripping down the sides. Tiny cans of tuna, that's what I see, along with some blue and black spots that fade in and out. My face hurts everywhere. I see Sonny's hand poised to wallop me again but for some reason it freezes in mid-air, inches from my face.

It seems he might be thinking something, a guy who has probably never had one thought in his entire life. Then he snorts, laughs, pats me on the shoulder. "You've got balls, kid," he says, and walks away as if nothing's happened. "See you around."

I'm sweating, trembling, but take the chance. "Hey, Sonny," I shout, "did you know that one speck of plutonium in the air would kill all of us."

Sonny whips his massive, crew-cut head around and smiles, beaming with health and raw voltage. "Huh?" he asks.

"Nothing," I wave.

He shoots a fist into the air and winks. "Tomorrow it's two quarters."

I lean back again, sink to my knees. I'm proud to have balls though they feel wilted and shriveled. Who needs plutonium when Sonny Busso's on the prowl? Tomorrow? It's always tomorrow. Plutonium just doesn't rate, not in this fun house.

Easter

We gather at the wooden table, spread with Belgian hand-stitched lace, a lead crystal bowl full of wet grapes at the center, and we wait, we wait for grandmother to return from the kitchen, a crypt of rosemary, sweet basil and garlic. The screen door keeps out the butterflies but not the pungent wafts of confederate jasmine, which nudge us like soft fists. Kisses. We wait for grandmother and her salver of lost bread, the small green pitcher of La Cuite, the powered sugar and slivers of iced strawberries.

As we have always gathered on this holy day. For grandmother. And as we wait, we watch each other slowly, gently disappear into milky gauze, then mist, then light, we turn into light. We are the light, the life, the resurrection, the body, the flesh, the body, the edible flesh of our grandmother, who smiles, hobbles into the room with, surprise!, a platter of fried plantains, our favorite. She is time, she is creation.

We tear into the fruit with our teeth, tiny tombstones embedded in our gums. Our Father, you have misled us. We visit her grave. We have never visited her grave. For she is levity, a butterfly, the soul, breath of the ages, pneuma, the egg. Shafts of sunlight break through the tall French shutters as we feast, bleaching us invisible.

Our grandmother arrives with a bowl of glazed caramel flan. "Wait til you taste it!" she gushes. We dig in, stuff ourselves and pray, fade again into light, the luminous cream flooding this eternal moment when we laugh and gossip and talk small above the clanks of pots and pans in the kitchen.

Mardi Gras Beads

Forgotten in the attic, heaped in dusty boxes, heavy glass beads, not the plastic doodads of today, the ones worth money, worth money, tags that say Czechoslovakia, that's what you want, Czechoslovakia, snatched from the air fifty years ago when parade floats burgeoned from the street, when they paused before us waiting like beggars, and masked revelers drunk and savage aim straight for your face, to hurt you, maim you because you're so damned greedy, scrambling for cheap Slavic trinkets, black flambeaus with fiery crosses propped in leather pouches twirling in the street, shadows from the Age of Myth bearing molten Jesus on a thousand crosses while someone glides a knife into your kidney because you jumped higher, pulled the beads right out of his fingers, the string snaps, glass splatters everywhere into horse shit on the street, puke, smashed tamales, no one gets anything now, no bulging pockets to empty and gloat...

We crowd at the rear of St. Louis Cathedral on Royal Street, the good street, safe, expensive antiques, decorous, unlike Bourbon one block over with naked bodies flung into gutters, the Cathedral so austere, lighted with blue mercury, doused in oils of sweet olive, Confederate jasmine, honey suckle, the garden of statues, Saint Panic, Saint Despair, Saint Madness, racked martyrs punctured with arrows and spears, petrified into porous alabaster down the years this one night, Comus Momus, who can remember? the float, a massive Poseidon with trident and sudsy waves, its krewe reeling hips obscenely, licking their lips, arms draped with the half-century later expensive beads, one drunk sequined phantom looks you in the eye through slit holes, pointing, these are for you, aims, winds his arm like a pitcher and instantly you bear the glittery load, beads beads beads, sewn together in a cluster, pressed against your chest so no one can yank away, you look back to signal thanks, the float lurches...

...He slips off Poseidon like a sack of feathers, floats to the asphalt, head wedged under the tractor's steel wheel, the uproar subsides, Mardi Gras silent as a tomb now as the wheel crushes his skull, the ghastly resonant crack, gray yellowish mush spilling out of his ears and mouth before your eyes in the front row, Saint Horror, Saint Massacre, and you shriek, pant, can't stop screaming howling, they come to sweep him away and Comus Momus proceeds, the crowd roaring, Throw me something Mister, hands fingering the air like fleshy wheat in a field, you've already got your stash, they lead you out of the throng in leaden shock, Make way, you hear, Make way, the sweaty push through bodies, driving home on deserted streets, Esplanade, Elysian Fields with its string of new sodium lights, the city phosphorescent eerie quiet subdued the midnight before Lent, atonement and sackcloth, Saint Desolation, Saint Trauma, still clutching the necklaces, his masked face, slit eyes, *these are for you,* bones cracked like a Zulu coconut, whacking it with a hammer, the beads, packed in shoe boxes...

Slid into a dark dusty attic until someone pulls them out, look at this, the good ones, listen, these will bring money, don't throw them away, Saint Dread, Saint Death, you can't get them anymore, any more, any more, and your powdery gnarled old fingers touch, rub beads you can't get any more, that will bring money, you mumble, remember, mumble, Saint Good Luck or Bad, Saint Time, Saint All-the-Dead-Ones, Saint Money, Saint Memory, full of grace, full of mercy, Saint All of Us.

Religious Experience

We had suffered through Luther's small catechism every day after school for months, and learned, first, that we were depraved and, second, that we would be punished for our depravity. It was a bad season. Signs of my own personal wretchedness abounded. On one occasion, for instance, I'd dropped my Luther into a pile of dog mess as I slouched to Pastor Hoffman's dismal class. I was beside myself. How could I show my face when my catechism effused such rankness? Surely everyone would notice.

It meant being late, but I rushed home and wiped every page with Dr. Tichenor's antiseptic. My mother supplied some potent perfume. By the time I got to class the little blue book reeked not with caca but *My Sin*. No one seemed to care. But I, miserable I, could still sniff the ordure behind the sweetness. On this day, oddly enough, Pastor Hoffman chose to tell us that when the Devil came to Martin Luther, Luther smelled him: and that smell was of excrement.

Weeks passed, and we memorized the appropriate sacraments, articles and creeds—anything, that is, Pastor Hoffman thought would make us more worthy of our certain damnation. He was a huge, dour German who never smiled, and did not hesitate to smack our knuckles with a wooden ruler if we failed to get our passages just right. We hated him, which made us feel all the more guilty since he was, after all, a man of God. Did God, I wondered secretly, approve of whacking kids with rulers? I was Italian and should have been Catholic anyway. I envied Catholic kids with a passion. They wore uniforms. God seemed to forgive them more easily. And they had all those saints to beseech.

When the final practice for both Confirmation and Communion arrived, we all took our places on the platform in front of the altar, Pastor Hoffman presiding with the zeal of a grand inquisitor. Our mothers sat in the first few pews wearing those goofy smiles not seen since the 1950s. We all knew all would probably go well enough except for Orville, the really bad kid who got more raps than anybody. Orville just might screw up the group recital all right. Pastor Hoffman kept a stern eye glued on Orville.

Little did I expect that it would be I, shy, depraved, wretched I, who would in fact ruin our practice and probably go straight to Hell for it. I stood there anonymously in the middle row—-how account for it? I became feverishly, inexplicably aroused. You know how that goes with twelve-year-old boys. There is no stopping it. Woe unto me, I nearly wept, I have defiled the very house of God. I am indeed the greatest of sinners, an agent of Satan. My catechism still reeked, however more gently, of the vileness I'd failed to scrub out of it as I held it in front of my disgrace.

Again, my only hope was that no one had noticed, for by the time we'd finished, I'd gone back to normal. To this day I wonder what could have inspired my ardor. Was it Becky McAdoo's blond perfumed hair, strands of which brushed across my face as we stood reciting the Sacrament of the Keys? Or was it something more ominous, my defiance of God and church and Pastor Hoffman and raps on the knuckles and Martin Luther's solemn injunctions against lust? Or was I simply irredeemably bad, *the* malefactor and saboteur set loose among our congregation.

When I stepped down from the altar and was led out of the church, my mother looked down at me with rare malice and hissed, "Don't you ever do that again." I was crushed. I 'd been discovered! And by my own mother! Lucky for me, she never mentioned the incident again.

But now, decades later, I know only too well that such moments are both our defeat and our glory, that the Devil had both tempted and inspired me with a gift beyond understanding, and that, yes—what a relief—it was good.

St. Picou's Bakery

Their first stop was the homey corner bakery with its bright clunky Coke machine and a pedestaled glass dome full of colored gum balls. Nickel drinks in aqua bottles, some frozen solid, shot out of a metal hole, and one of Rudi Grousse's pennies bought a handful of gum balls that fizzled like acid when slipped into a bulging mouthful of Coke. On King's Day the cousins waited in line for a ringed cake glazed with the colors of Mardi Gras, a cake that looked like one of the newly discovered galaxies Jake had seen in Meme's *National Geographic*. "Be careful not to crack your teeth," his grandmother always warned, since each cake contained a tiny bisque doll or maybe a whole pecan, a tradition celebrating the ancient Bean King, or Lord of Misrule. Meme had known a young man who split a molar on one of the pecan shells, but he put off going to Dr. Muniere, and soon the tooth abscessed and his blood turned to puss. Meme said his last words were "Never eat king cake." But cracked teeth didn't mean a thing to Jake and his cousins and they devoured the festive slabs of dough with little heed to the story about the unlucky young man. Bad luck happened to other people.

Closer to Easter the smell of hot cross buns wafted all the way to Columbus Street in fog-like tendrils of temptation. Jake, though, preferred the gooey macaroons Ruthie said tasted like turpentine; the dense jelly rolls that crumbled when touched, spongy lady fingers which swelled like a lizard's throat if smeared with a single drop of saliva. Ruthie favored eclairs and Napoleons, both putrid and off limits to her brother.

Meme went crazy over the pound cake, a mystery to her grandson who dismissed pound cake as the most boring dessert on earth. "Try this," Meme would close her eyes and smile, "it's out of this world. Mr. Picou told me it comes from a recipe in his family since the days when France was still Gaul. He makes it with twenty-seven sticks of butter." Jake didn't care if the pound cake came from Mesopotamia, a place way older than Gaul.

Yet there were some products everyone loved—fluffy glazed donuts or those slushy with vanilla or chocolate cream, cinnamon rolls and steaming French bread with brittle crust. No one in the entourage ever left Picou's without carrying a white paper bag full of such pastries and hot bread. Rumors that the Board of Health was about to shut the bakery down because dogs and cats and pigeons roamed freely on the premises alarmed the entire neighborhood.

Two or three cats were always pruning on the massive wooden table where the bakers spread and kneaded dough, and loose flour clogging the air had turned them, and the bakers as well, into bleached ghosts of themselves. One patron found a still living pigeon inside the sponge cake she bought for her husband's birthday. The delighted husband consumed both cake and pigeon in one marathon splurge. "Pigeons are doves," he exclaimed, "so I've eaten the Holy Ghost! I'm shriven!" City inspectors also objected to the green mold that coated the brick walls of the bakery, but Mr. Picou claimed it had medicinal properties, and he often scraped off a bit and added it to the dough of pastries destined for customers who were ill. "I've cured more sick people in this city than any doctor," he liked to boast, and his patrons agreed, some pronouncing him Dr. or St. Picou. "I can tell by the eyes who's got what," he said. "The one those youngsters call Meme. I put extra collagen in her donuts. She's got lupus but doesn't know it, or rather, she knows it in her blood but keeps it secret. Passes it off as rheumatism. Close me down and lots of people will suffer."

Mr. Picou vowed to fight this mysterious non-entity called The Board of Heath, which seemed to consist entirely of writs from lawyers and perhaps a sole inspector in black suit arriving every so often. He placed full page ads in the *Times-Picayune* demanding the rights of people to enjoy doughnuts; he appeared on radio talk shows; he paid for billboards that portrayed his smiling face as he bit into a bulging cinnamon roll; he formed rallies on Bayou Road calling for the abolition of the Board of Health; and, more furtively, he mailed photos of a black hand to members of the city council, even the mayor. He had dipped his own hand into a bucket of black paint and persuaded Paw to photograph it with his Leica. Paw made fifty copies of the black hand and delivered them to Mr. Picou in exchange for a crate of Italian bread. "I'll take this to the limit," he swore to Paw, and Paw agreed he should. Otherwise, where would it end? But Paw tempered his support a bit when Mr. Picou erected a massive wooden cross on one of the bakery's outside walls. "Picou is crazy," he informed the family. "That's a bougalie for you."

News about Picou blitzed through the neighborhood like rogue voltage. Its doors had been closed forever by the accursed Board of Health, and collective wails arose from the neighborhood as prayers of grief. Mr. Picou had tied himself to the wooden cross and hung there day and night, declaring himself a sacrificial victim of City Hall. Liberato was stunned; Violet sobbed; the cousins threw rocks at the NO TRESPASSING sign; Meme sighed as she twiddled what was left of her arthritic thumbs; the pews of St. Rosa de Lima were packed, not only with people but even the stray spectral cats that Mr. Picou had kept well fed.

Within three days two black NOPD squad cars arrived to remove Mr. Picou from the cross. They arrested him for indecent exposure and making a public nuisance of himself, for he ranted and spat upon passersby dressed in a black suit. He fought the police who lugged him down, crying, "It is finished." No one ever saw Mr. Picou again, but rumors abounded that his relatives had committed him to the Home for the Incurables, a place, it seems, every person in New Orleans had good reason to dread, a diffuse apprehension that certainly did not spare young Jake who cringed at the mere word *Incurable*.

Adultery

Geneviève sweeps in breathlessly, wild-eyed, hair flared out, her gorgeous lips quivering, her hands waving in every direction, as I await her in the darkest corner of The Napoleon House.

"He followed me!" she cries from across the room, approaching my table laden with a crock of gumbo and a few empty shot glasses of chartreuse. Every head in the house turns toward us at the news. "He said he was going to kill you, break every bone in your body!"

My heart palpitates and I leap forward, push away the table, as I see Mick bulldoze his way through a crowd of cheerful Iowans clustered at the front door. I whisk Geneviève out another side door onto Chartres Street, and, clutching her hand, nearly lug her across the pavement. I was once a high school sprinter on the track team—even earned a letter or two—so I knew how to skedaddle. I am almost dragging Geneviève behind me.

"Wait," she huffs, "he can't run fast right now, he hurt his foot yesterday. Slow down, please, Cecci." Yep, she calls me Cecci, not Marcus; everybody calls me Cecci, which in Italian, means a kind of chickpea. Perhaps a sad omen but I take the good news about Mick's foot as opportunity to duck around a corner and slip through an open wrought iron patio door into a courtyard lush with foliage.

We squeeze behind a rear stand of bamboo, each stalk rising into the dark liquid sky like a stirring rod. Between an ancient brick wall and the bamboo stand I press Geneviève against the bricks and waste no time unbuttoning her blouse and cupping her breasts, kissing her all over, ah, the spice of danger arousing us both to unchartered heights of passion. Who am I kidding? Everything is chartered long before the likes of us arrived on the scene. But the intensity, spiked with potent aphrodisiacs of fear and desire, feels detonative enough as soldier after soldier promptly arises.

We hear Mick pass outside the wall wailing his wife's name, a piteous and forlorn grovel. "Gen, I'm sorry, Gen" he coughs and growls, "I won't hurt him. Come back, baby, come back." As he approaches Decatur one street over the grunts and screams diminish elegantly, the way a bad dream fades. Stanley Kowalski dissolving. I might feel sorry for him if only he weren't deranged with an intent to kill.

"He's lying," Geneviève pants as I grope her, as she gropes me, "he knows where you live, he did research. You're kind of famous too, you know. People know you. They read your work in the papers. I should go home."

"No," I pound my skull with two fists, "He'll kill you." Her words both incense and terrify me.

"He just wants me back. He would never hurt me. He cries all the time now, writes me long letters, begs me not to leave him. I feel terrible and guilty and ashamed but I shouldn't. He has one girlfriend after another. I must go home tonight so he won't kill himself, that is, before he finds and kills you first. Don't go back to your apartment tonight, please, please. Oh, I love you so much. I want you. I can't stop thinking about you."

Another soldier arises. Those words in the heat of perilous longing and craving… Anything better in this malfunctioning universe?

"I love you too, I love you," and now I'm crying and she's crying and Mick's crying and everybody alive is crying and maybe the dead are crying. And though Geneviève and I have met secretly for a few months now we have never consummated our union.She is a very respectable, cautious, terrified young woman, only twenty-two, to my thirty-two, but tonight, ah, tonight I lay us down between a brick wall built during the regime of Alejandro O'Reilly (the brutal yet efficient Spanish governor who hanged insurrectionists in Jackson Square as examples for all) and the clacking bamboo and we make love madly, a mazurka, then again slowly, lente, an adagio, then the mazurka again, the adagio, imagine, on the mud between a brick wall and bamboo stalks! We spend ourselves in this dizzying, impetuous fashion and finally, wrapped in each other's arms, we doze off trying to catch our breaths as an owl hoots in one of the crepe myrtles across the courtyard.

Before Mick caught on to me Geneviève would follow me after class as I led the way to the batture of old Carrollton, once a separate city. We would walk hand in hand and talk.

I felt she was probing me, getting a feel for who exactly I was, and, ditto, I the same with her. She had attended classy schools, Ecole Classique and Newman, where all the rich, privileged kids go as opposed to my shoddy McDonogh public schools over in the Bayou Road area. Her father is a psychiatrist at some uptown institution, and before she married Mick she lived in what I can only describe as a palatial estate in a gated Audubon community off St. Charles. Why she chose to enroll at the sleazy lakefront campus I hesitated to ask but figured it had something to do with getting away from Mick for a breather.At first she had difficulty saying anything at all (a red flag?), to speak, and actual lumps formed in her throat when she responded to any question I might ask; she seemed pathologically shy and reserved which I rightly or wrongly dismissed as elegance, the province of royalty, the Jackie Kennedy stalwart stoneface at JFK's funeral. Another red flag? I sensed she was making up her mind about me, deciding whether I amounted to friend or foe and whether or not I deserved a bestowal of any kind. A non-risk taker, Geneviève had crossed her own line by preparing to take one of the biggest risks in her life.

I craved those walks with her, longed to embrace her but intuited that this would be no easy, loose courtship but rather old school, high style, troubadour wooing, an ordeal I would endure for no other person on earth. That's how much she means to me. I am also impressed by the intelligence and refined prose of the essays she writes in and out of my class. One of them I read over and over again. It's called "When I'm Dead." Ah, a melancholic woman into Thanatos! (She wrote that she would find it peaceful!) Of course, she received no grade lower than A.

Soon enough I am walking Geneviève back to her dinky Renault parked down by Jackson Barracks, a car bestowed upon her by her father when he bought a new Mazda, and after tearful parting and suffocating hugs she starts the ignition—we can't stop kissing each other, she in the driver's seat, I outside leaning in—but she finally pulls from the curb and drives back uptown to her abode with Mick. I didn't press her on her plans; she seemed too distressed, too agitated, to beset with guilt to discuss any future with me.

So it's back to the agony of waiting, waiting to see her again, waiting for her to leave her husband, waiting for her to resolve her anxieties and face the brute (well, Mick is no brute, he merely seeks to reconcile with his wife, his wife after all). I too would have fought for her. Hell, that's what I'm doing now.

Tyler Avenue

As I walk along, I wonder what went wrong…
—Del Shannon

This morning on my way to 7-11 for twenty ounces of muddy French Roast I drove up Tyler Avenue and passed a fistful of rowdy adolescent boys cavorting, whooping, putting on a show.

One of them sternly catapulted then spun down with a sharp knuckle clip to the clavicle of his punier buddy. The victim crumpled, shot back, howled, and laughing again, stormed his friend

with a barrage of vengeful kicks in the ass. All this as I passed, you see, taking it in. I'd forgotten such robust camaraderie the wide-mouthed guffaws, as if to saunter down a dreary street and expect nothing less than romping good times are natural as grass.

How could they register the slow shadow of my drab gray Saturn, my wispy hair, or know my back had sabotaged itself again as I squirmed on a bucket seat in pain so persistent it assumed material form, belted itself into shotgun, and resumed the otiose dialectic of whether or not we must suffer to savor pleasure—in a word, does alpha need omega? But philosophic worms had long since fled any sizzling beach I long to tread; "No contest," I cried, as harpoons impaled my least enlightened chakra, Abdomen. I too would not have noticed myself.

Clouded with vodka, codeine and Ativan I lean back on a buzzing heating pad and watch Regis Philbin, the same emcee my dying grandmother watched years ago—Regis, the everlasting last resort. For pure relief I summoned up those boys, their faces smeared with levity, their muscles rippling like oil as they strutted, pranced, groped… toward what? a ball game? pool hall? girls? Minor mischief in the works was clear.

Which brought to mind another raucous group crammed like junk in a crimson Plymouth Valiant. We sped up Elysian Fields screeching "Runaway," boasted how far each of us had got with Mary Ann Diebeau, chanted the cheers of Bear Bryant's Crimson Tide until we reached the humped stone bridge of City Park, the only local mound sedans could span at such an angle that all four whitewalls spun in air. Vertigo in the guts, we wanted it. I can't see our faces anymore, only gaping mouths, the same whoops, squeals and shenanigans as the Tyler gang that instant we dangled in space.

What did we find so exhilarating, so fun? Just being together, young? Knowing we couldn't die? Not exactly knowing, for death made no entry at the time, assumed no posture in the equation. We were pure occasion. Nothing to do, nowhere to go—we battered each other and laughed at our wounds, the ridiculous bridge, the Valiant as it rumbled down; we seized pleasures bloated like roses in a garden bed. Jan's dead a decade now, Phil thickened a bit, Jim, alas, a lawyer, Hereford, vanished in Alabama, with wife, kids, all the drowsy accouterments of grace. And I, losing spine and strands of hair, sit stiffly upon the sofa I inherited from my grandmother.

So to the boys on Tyler Avenue, I bid good cheer though well I know that one of you will someday stoop to pick up keys and feel your entrails rip, a strip of cartilage or powdery disc, and sense that while your life is not quite over, it surely hobbles up another street. And you, destined first to die, I pray you will have purged your final laugh by then, since laughs, like tears, are staunchly finite. But I'm not crying yet. Drugged, half-paralyzed for a while, I can still manage a bittersweet smile. Oh Regis, funny old clown, how soon we inch into the hungry, yawping, saw-toothed ground.

Mary

I'm wild about this girl Mary and we spend every night and sometimes afternoons despoiling each other grandly and she's so beautiful I have to hold back lest I decompose on the spot because no man can contain such beauty and I regret now, the hesitation, but when you're twenty-five what do you know? And one splendid eve full of locusts and sweet olive she insists I meet her parents (not in the cards, parents, not back then) and I say ok and we drive out to the lakefront to this modest (I could say shitty) clapboard and trot up the steps and she swings open the door and the mother has gone off to Maison Blanche but there's the dad, this frail, bald, withered guy slouched on a plaid sofa behind a fold-out wooden table full of mid-term exams because he's a math professor at the local and they need grading... can't say he likes the looks of me and surely he knows everything.

I mean, how would you feel? But the whammy comes later when she tells me he's dying of brain cancer and my heart catapults because here we are driving along St. Charles Avenue past all the mansions, headed for the Quarter, The Napoleon house, where they make mediocre Ramos Gin Fizzes and shrimp po-boys because we need some energy and power for what will become an all-nighter back in my apartment on Ursulines and Dauphine, but this whole time I'm thinking about that guy, dying, his brain devoured, and she said the chemo makes him nauseous and weak and didn't kill the pain much, and there he sat grading math problems, and weakly I laugh, "It doesn't add up, why bother?"

And she says he is a conscientious man and starts to cry and I pull her over beside me and stroke her sizzling hair and know the passion will be more sacred than ever and fear I might not hold back and thereby lose myself to her grief, and I know it's wrong but I curse the dying man and all mathematics, and the university and the universe, and myself, and her, I curse everyone because we're cursed anyway and it all amounts to a few drops of Tabasco in cold waxen broth.

Squalls

1. Frills of the Mind

"He who rises late must trot all day," Magdalena sighs. She is rubbing the Helsinki Hair Rejuvenation Formula into her scalp as I shuffle into the room, my feet spilling out of a pair of rancid corduroy slippers I'd found in her closet. Magdalena is not going bald; she wants *fierce* hair, she says, viscous, the envy of all. Her hair has acquired a sort of ultramarine tint and looks mean enough to attack something.

"Who said that about trotting? I know somebody said that," I ask, still groggy from the Chablis of last night, enhanced by my addiction to Librium as well as the Benadryl in my system. The latter eases a poison oak rash I'd picked up after foolishly traipsing through the wilderness in one of my rare bursts of nature worship. I'm not a wilderness person. I knew I'd catch something or be eaten or get hopelessly lost.

Magdalena starts to pour the Formula onto her scalp.

"That stuff burns when it gets into a cut," I say. "I tried it after you conked out last night. As you see, it didn't work."

"Benjamin Franklin. You flunked."

She refers to our little habit, surely out of hand by now, of testing each other with famous or not so famous quotes. At first an official game, it now verges on warfare. One of us shoots out a quote and the other has to identify it. The more craftily we disguise it in our conversation, the greater the stakes. I decide to give her a break.

"Try this: *What you fear most is what will happen.*"

When she turns her arm knocks the end table and the small brown Helsinki jar crashes to the floor. "Oh, Jesus, one hundred bucks down the tubes. My floorboards will sprout hair."

"Helsinki's stock has shot way up. Did you buy any?"

"I don't believe in stock," she says, wiping up the Formula with a bath towel that had been draped around her shoulder. Otherwise, she is absolutely, vividly naked—some sight, at noon. Bent over, her breasts still seem to rise skyward, and she catches me glancing.

Louis Gallo

"All you want is my body."

"No," I cleared my throat, "what I really want is your mind. To penetrate your mind would be fabulous."

"Penetrate."

"Yes, the ultimate copula."

"You think a lot about that sort of thing, don't you? I mean, your organ and all that. I suppose that's because it looms so."

The Formula seems to lift the Minwax right off Magdalena's floorboards. It has, at any rate, formed this splotchy white stain beside the sofa.

"Oh, look at this," Magdalena cries, "my knotholes are ruined."

I do a little entrechat, hoping it will make me seem more magnetic than I feel. I have this theory about people who execute entrechats and somersaults or pirouettes in public: they lack energy, and are embarrassed, so they compensate.

"So who said it?"

"Caesar Pavase. Italian."

"I've given up on reading. I'm into direct experience now."

"*Into*? Did you say *into*?"

"All words are created equal."

"Well, excuse me," I say, flapping about like Steve Martin as I hobble out of the room. Last night when I met her at Flanagan's, Magdalena was just the thing: bright, svelte, incisive, decisive, passionate, witty, beyond fad and foible. Now I feel I've been used for her transitory pleasure and want to smash something.

"*I* am not *into* transitory pleasures," I shout from the bathroom as I gather my lens case and saline solution, my moustache wax and brush. I see no point in extending our relationship. Naturally, I pocket the loose change Magdalena keeps atop her toilet tank. While at it I filch her most valuable cosmetics and a pair of Marx scissors.

2. Bleeps of the Heart

It was neither day nor night outside. I knew I had left Magdalena's around noon, but I cannot account for the hours between. I found myself on the street, duffel bag slung over my shoulder, attaché case dangling from my fingers. When the old lady passed—we were deeply entrenched in the Central Business District (Magdalena lived clear across town)—she looked me in the eye and whispered "squalls."

I glanced over to where she pointed. The bit of sky I could see did indeed contain a raw, black swatches which I assumed were squalls. They seemed stationed above the lake at the moment, but no telling how soon they would move in and destroy power lines, windows, trees and even some people. I decided to seek refuge. I remembered that bit of advice from an old Civil Defense pamphlet: seek refuge.

I wandered into the Pere Marquette Building, which, as usual, smelled of prescription drugs, and set my bags against the wall under the attorney directory. An old janitor found me sitting on the art deco tiles manicuring my fingernails.

"May I inquire as to your business, suh?" he asked deferentially as he brushed debris off my shoulders with his little whisk broom. How quaint, I thought, here is a man who knows how to treat strangers. He was the color of parchment and had a grin that seemed stapled to his face.

"Squalls," I said, assuming we shared terror if nothing else.

"Yep," he grinned. "But dis here ain't no haven, no. Dis here's a privit building. I got to ax you to leave. Ain't you got no home, no lovin' wife wit soft long arms, no nice white family? Ain't you got no preciousness? How long you been bald?"

We stepped out into the weather to watch the sky rearrange itself. His questions were a kind of execution, unlike the questions Magdalena and I asked one another. No, I suddenly realized with a shock, I don't have a loving wife with soft long arms, a nice white family, a preciousness.

"No preciousness!" I screeched. "Only Magdalena with green hair, and I invented her to have something to do, someone to be with, somewhere to go. There's no Magdalena."

I actually trembled now as the janitor held me in his arms. "Dem squalls be furious," he said, "always like dat. Way back in history in the time of Darius and Jewels Caesar and Great Kong dey be squalls. Squalls is the lonely heart of man crying for itself. Nothin' but sadness, nothin' but nothin'."

I jerked free, recoiled from my comforter.

"That's monstrous! Get away from me. Judas! Infidel!"

The rain swept over the city in blinding, angry sheets. The janitor disappeared, vanished altogether in the gathering maelstrom, and I had no choice but to find my car and rush back to Magdalena before I too vanished. Up to that point I had only imagined myself, and perhaps not

Louis Gallo

so vividly, but as I drove through the pelting rain, sobbing, pounding the dashboard like a savage, I felt remarkably alive, as if birth meant little more than sincere recognition and acceptance of infinite loss.

Gender

The conversation had started as fun but was now depressing Lisa. How has she borne me and my troubles?

"Love is blind," she finally sighed.

"Good," I smacked the table, "then nothing can ever be said on the subject by anyone at any time. We've reached the impasse of impasses. Love is blind. Let's find ourselves a pair of kindly seeing-eye dogs."

"I'm not laughing, not even smiling."

"Look, you're going at this all wrong. You're assuming I'm a man. I'm not. I'm a woman. I'm a woman who happens to be a man. All those things women do like show their emotions, discuss personal problems, have maternal instincts, feather their nests—I'm like that. I'm the one who snuggled Lanie, not Rachel. I'd like to stay home and dust the whatnot and sign up as home room mother. What a deal! The old hubby out there grinding away for paychecks while you stay put and test the latest kitchen tile spray. What's so great about being a man? I'll tell you what men do. This is men. They get together and dig big holes in the ground. They take little breaks and stare into the sun, sling the shovels over their shoulders as they chug beer, maybe belch some whoppers before the digging starts again. Then they've got this big hole. But they can't stand it, so they sort of sneak out in the moonlight and gather round the hole. They don't say anything because the hole's almost sacred. WE DUG THIS. They just hang around. Every so often one will measure the hole to make sure it's still deep. Somebody will say, "Yep." The others will nod, maybe spit into the hole. Then they go home and maybe hump the old lady. But they're really thinking about that hole.

"Would women spend their time hanging around holes going "Yep." Another thing. I saw this flatbed truck hauling a giant piece of machinery on the interstate the other day. Who knows what the machine was for? It has massive gears and shafts and all sorts of bearings. I'm sure it had bearings. Men love bearings. Grommets too, whatever they are. Anyway, if women ran the show this machine would never been invented. Women wouldn't want it. No big holes, no stupid machines.

Women would leave the earth alone. "Or have you ever seen women hanging around service stations? It's only men who wear those overalls with grease coated into their atomic structures. Women sip daiquiris at Houlihan's or pick out bisque figurines in some boutique Men are so stupid they haven't figured out what's going on. I love women. I love them because I'm one myself. Being a woman doesn't threaten my manhood; it enhances it. I'm proud to be a woman."

Lisa stared at me, a bit stunned, I think. I get carried away sometimes. I slurped the cold coffee and waited.

"That was some spiel," she sighed. She sucked an ice cube out of her glass of ice tea and crushed it with her teeth. "So you have a vagina, eh?"

"Sure, why not?"

"I thought so."

Off the Road

So I'm back in the car, parked close to the only old-fashioned phone booth left in America, out in the middle of nowhere at this filling station, the only such establishment for the last thirty miles. I'm eating a sandwich and sipping fresh coffee roasted directly from ground beans when suddenly there comes a rap on my half-rolled up window. The driver of this monster vehicle idling on a patch of grass beyond the pumps.

"Got change for a fin, buddy?" the driver asks. He looks middle-aged and wiry with worrisome facial erosion and scar tissue across his cheeks and forehead. A fine golden silt covers every inch of his body as if he happened to be in close proximity to some heavy-duty sanding. Wears a ten-gallon hat with an oval portrait of J.E.B. Stuart affixed to the denim pocket of his work shirt. "Got to call the old lady."

"Yeah, let me check," I say, rooting around in my bag. "I can just give you two quarters if that's all you need. No big deal. But I was here first and need to call Wendy, my wife, you know."

"Nosuh," the driver waves, "don't take nothin from nobody. Bad policy, right? Then you wind up owing. Me, I don't owe nothin and I'm keepin it that way."

"Ok, but I don't think I have change"—I'm frantically searching, believe me—"so I might have to give you the quarters anyway."

The man seemed mortally offended. "Nosuh," he repeated, "don't take no quarters for nothing. I ain't no parasite. Worked all my life so I could say, me, Kyle Brister don't take nothing from nobody. Now, son, you jus git me that change."

I'm worried now. That last sentence verged on threat. Out here in the darkness it's only me and this eroded Kyle Brister and the filling station cashier, a rather overweight short lady with peroxided hair seriously into bronchial disorder and crosswords. The earth could explode and crossword addicts would still look up in a daze to ask if you know a three-letter word for barbed wire.

"Well," I say to Kyle, "I guess we're at an impasse. I don't have change but I have two quarters. You won't take the quarters because it would make you a parasite. What do we do?"

Kyle Brister scratches his chin and spits a wad of brownish fluid from his mouth into the shrubbery beside the booth. "It's only that you gotta call the old lady for me, that would make it all right, I guess," he sighs. "You call the old lady and use your quarters, then I ain't no parasite and you go free. Cause the only option is I gotta rob you. You don't give me no other option, right? I mean if you ain't got change and all."

"Yeah?" I ask, "then how'd you plan to pay for the gas that's being pumped into your truck at this very moment."

"Got credit," he says proudly, "I'm American. Got a Shell card when I was twenty-five and had it ever since. I pay my bills, yesuh. But sometimes a man needs to rob another man to call his old lady."

Do I want to call Kyle Brister's old lady? I haven't even finished my sandwich. I consider arguing but Kyle looks like a man who would have no trouble wasting me and then demolishing the entire station to destroy evidence, so I get out, the disputed quarters between my fingers, and deposit them into the slot. Someone has scratched the name Ethel into the black paint on the phone.

"What's the number?" I ask.

"Dunno," he says, "got to call the operator down in Pulaski County."

"You don't know your own telephone number?" I ask.

"Why should I know that? Ain't we got enough to know without knowing something like that? You just dial information and get that Pulaski operator and say you want the telephone number of Dolly Brister down in Hillsville."

Mine is not to reason why, so I connect with the operator, get the number and dial, Kyle Brister looking on with nodding approval. The phone rings for quite a while.

"You let it ring. Takes Dolly some time to answer if she's watching a program. Might have to wait for the commercial."

So I let it ring and ring, and finally a throaty, effluvial "yeah?" comes my way. I must say I'm impressed. I'd expected a chirp or squeak. What a voice on Dolly in Hillsville.

"You say Kyle is calling from he don't know where and wants to tell her everything's fine and how is Scooter?" Kyle says.

"Uh," I say, "Kyle is calling from he don't know where and wants to tell you everything's fine and how is Scooter?"

"Who is this?" Dolly asks, more than a little puzzled.

"This is Jake, you don't know me—calling for Kyle because he doesn't want to be a parasite, which he would be if he took my quarters."

"Put the moron on," she orders.

"She wants to talk to you," I offer the phone to Kyle.

No no no, he waves his hands.

"He won't talk," I say.

"Tell that jerk he ain't using your quarters no more, that this conversation is being paid for on this end by me."

This I do and add, "Kyle, Dolly has a point. You only used my money for the Hillsville operator." I reach into the slot to retrieve them. "See?" I beam, "here they are. Dolly's paying for the call now and that means you aren't a parasite."

Kyle scratches his head and deposits more brownish liquid into the shrubbery. "Lemme think about it," he mumbles. "Yeah, I guess that's so. Ok, podner, you done your duty, now get lost so I can talk to my woman in private."

I hold the phone at arm's length. "Kyle, I hope you don't plan to talk long. I was here first and I want to call my woman too. Somebody ripped the headpiece from the other phone. Fair's fair."

"Gimme ten minutes," he almost pleads. "Then you can come back and talk to your woman. I ain't seen Dolly for two weeks and I'm crazy about her, and me and her got to talk. You understand?"

Of course I understand. I admire Kyle immensely at the moment and would have waited hours until he finished to shake his hand. I imagine Dolly another Wendy comforting her soul mate in his time of troubles. He seems the kind of man trouble clings to like algae. You don't worry about owing someone when life spreads easy as whipped cream. So I return to the Trooper to finish my sandwich, which, let me confess, I suspect will lay me low with ptomaine. I could wind up in a motel two or three hours from now doubled over with agonizing spasms and no one would know. Next day the maid would find me, shriek and I'd wind up being rolled up in a sheet and carried out by county deputies. Another small ignominious possibility. Thank God, small ignominious possibilities no longer distress me; and I have ceased fantasizing about glorious cremation upon a Viking ship or leaping into an erupting volcano, making, that is, a spectacle of my adieu. You could say I've mellowed. Wrapped in a squalid Motel 6 sheet is fine with me.

Kyle Brister finally finishes and before he gets into his truck, or whatever it is, I rush over to say goodbye. He seems startled to see me and rears back. "Whoaaa," he gasps, then, "oh, it's you." I notice he has tears in his eyes. "I don't owe you nothin," he waves me away and hoists himself onto his very high seat. "I'm done for, man," he screeches, "that woman's fixed me good. Gonna be the death of me."

"Just wanted to shake," I say ridiculously. "Are you ok? No, I guess you're not."

Now he really starts to bawl, clearing his eyes with his shirt sleeve. "Don't owe nobody nothin!" he howls ferociously, pumping the accelerator madly so that the roar of his engine makes further talk futile. He burns so much rubber out of the station they can probably smell it all the way to Fairfax. And thus ends my sole encounter with Kyle Brister, a dusty, aggrieved man whose hand I will never shake.

A Special Case

Blink. Blink. Blink. I blink my eyes. Over and over, little windows. If I hold my head back, I see Lizard hanging from the ceiling. They put me on this porch. Blink. Hello, Lizard. I will catch you and watch your pink throat puff up like cotton candy. You aren't afraid of me. Red Bean is a member of the Legume family. Red Bean Legume. Sal Paretti. Marie Paretti. Johnny Young. Sandy Young. The cousins. I know their names. They live around the corner. They call me Pinhead. Mommy told Telephone I came out of the womb wrong. They clamped my head with pliers. Blink. Hello, Telephone. Who are you now? My aunt Rosalie. I can't go anywhere, not to the park or school or the lake. I don't walk right, Mommy says, and can't read or write. I can't learn anything like continents or streets or words. Pliers squeezed my brains. Sofia is the capitol of Bulgaria. I make horrible sounds that scare people. Animal sounds. Lizard doesn't say anything, so I don't say anything. Lizard tells me secrets. So do Mosquito Hawk and Rat and Hummingbird. And Potato, Artichoke and Kumquat. Wood whispers to me. And Pewter Tankard from great grandma. Nails hold the house together. Air goes up, up, up. Moon comes down. Sometimes Moon is a fingernail. Rain is wet. I like rain music. Electricity is the flow of electrons from one pole to another. Electrons have negative charges. What is the capitol of Mars? Mom tells Telephone I'm hopeless. Dad drove away in a car named Studebaker and never came back. He went to Baton Rouge, capitol of Louisiana. Because of me, Mom tells Telephone. I don't remember him except his smell, which lingers. Dr. Tichenor's Antiseptic. It burns your eyes. Noun is the name of a person, place or thing. I am a noun. Mom cries and cries and cries. Cry is a verb. She doesn't hear Lizard say hello. She doesn't see Moon. She sits in the dark room. When I blink too much, she tells me to stop, it looks ugly. Ugly is an adjective. I have a name but it's secret. Sal, Marie, Johnny and Sandy call me Pinhead. They don't know my name. If they did, they would say hello, Name. They're not bad like the ones who throw rocks and call me Vegetable. Rocks belong to the Mineral family. Rocks say they are sorry to hurt me. All I do is rock on the swing.

Rock is a verb. And a noun. When I go inside I sit on the sofa. The sofa is brown. I like Sofa. It tickles me. Then I sleep and dream about Swing. I dream I swing into the sky and meet Angels. Angels have no bodies. Angels tell me hello. I do not blink. Sal went to Kindergarten today. Poor Sal. Lucky Sal. I will never go to Kindergarten because I'm hopeless. Lizard teaches me, Moon teaches, Sofa teaches. Spider too. I thank them. I love them. I am not afraid of me. I am not afraid of anything. Distance equals rate times time. Sometimes I see Sal walking home from school right behind Judy France. Judy has the name of a country. The capitol of France is Paris. Sal pants after Paris. Judy is so pretty I kiss her in my dreams. And she kisses me back. Dream loves me. Dream makes me better. Kindergarten is a dream of light. Nothing can travel faster than the speed of light.

Except me.

About the Author

Seven volumes of Louis Gallo's poetry, *Archaeology, Scherzo Furiant, Crash, Clearing the Attic, Ghostly Demarcation & The Pandemic Papers, Why Is There Something Rather than Nothing?* and *Leeway & Advent*. His work appears in Best Short Fiction 2020. A novella, "The Art Deco Lung," appears in *Storylandia*. National Public Radio aired a reading and discussion of his poetry on its "With Good Reason" series (December 2020). His work has appeared or will shortly appear in *Wide Awake in the Pelican State* (LSU anthology), *Southern Literary Review, Fiction Fix, Glimmer Train, Hollins Critic, Rattle, Southern Quarterly, Litro, New Orleans Review, Xavier Review, Glass: A Journal of Poetry, Missouri Review, Mississippi Review, Texas Review, Baltimore Review, Pennsylvania Literary Journal, The Ledge, storySouth, Houston Literary Review, Tampa Review, Raving Dove, The Journal* (Ohio), *Greensboro Review*, and many others. Chapbooks include *The Truth Changes, The Abomination of Fascination, Status Updates and The Ten Most Important Questions of the Twentieth Century.* He is the founding editor of the now defunct journals, *The Barataria Review* and *Books: A New Orleans Review*. His work has been nominated for the Pushcart Prize several times. He is the recipient of an NEA grant for fiction. He teaches at Radford University in Radford, Virginia. He is a native of New Orleans.

THE RE-ATTRIBUTION OF THE BRITISH RENAISSANCE CORPUS

ANNA FAKTOROVICH

MODERNIZATION OF THE INACCESSIBLE BRITISH RENAISSANCE

WILLIAM PERCY

SONNETS TO THE FAIREST COELIA

THREE LETTERS

ANNA FAKTOROVICH, TRANSLATOR

MODERNIZATION OF THE INACCESSIBLE BRITISH RENAISSANCE

WILLIAM PERCY

THE THIRSTY ARABIA

ANNA FAKTOROVICH, TRANSLATOR

MODERNIZATION OF THE INACCESSIBLE BRITISH RENAISSANCE

WILLIAM PERCY

FAIRY PASTORAL

ANNA FAKTOROVICH, TRANSLATOR

MODERNIZATION OF THE INACCESSIBLE BRITISH RENAISSANCE

WILLIAM PERCY

CUCK-QUEANS' AND CUCKOLDS' ERRANDS

ANNA FAKTOROVICH, TRANSLATOR

BRRAM

20-Volume Series

Proves with computational linguistics, handwriting and biographical analysis:

6 GHOSTWRITERS

Created All British Renaissance Texts

First translations of inaccessible books, with annotations, introductions

https://AnaphoraLiterary .com/Attribution

MODERNIZATION OF THE INACCESSIBLE BRITISH RENAISSANCE

WILLIAM PERCY

APHRODISIA

ANNA FAKTOROVICH, TRANSLATOR

MODERNIZATION OF THE INACCESSIBLE BRITISH RENAISSANCE

WILLIAM PERCY

FEDELE and FORTUNIO

ANNA FAKTOROVICH, TRANSLATOR

MODERNIZATION OF THE INACCESSIBLE BRITISH RENAISSANCE

RICHARD VERSTEGAN

RESTITUTION of DECAYED INTELLIGENCE

ANTIQUITIES

ANNA FAKTOROVICH, TRANSLATOR

MODERNIZATION OF THE INACCESSIBLE BRITISH RENAISSANCE

GABRIEL HARVEY

SMITH Or, The Tears of the Muses

ANNA FAKTOROVICH, TRANSLATOR

MODERNIZATION OF THE INACCESSIBLE BRITISH RENAISSANCE

WILLIAM PERCY

HAMLET The First Quarto

ANNA FAKTOROVICH, TRANSLATOR

MODERNIZATION OF THE INACCESSIBLE BRITISH RENAISSANCE

WILLIAM PERCY

FOREST TRAGEDY

ANNA FAKTOROVICH, TRANSLATOR

MODERNIZATION OF THE INACCESSIBLE BRITISH RENAISSANCE

WILLIAM PERCY

LOOK AROUND YOU

ANNA FAKTOROVICH, TRANSLATOR

www.ingramcontent.com/pod-product-compliance
Lightning Source LLC
Chambersburg PA
CBHW050347030726
47503CB00008B/2658